Whispers of the Flame

by Belinda Chavremootoo

Dedication

For the ones who remember, even when they are told to forget.

For the silenced, the seekers, and the storytellers.

And for the island—because land never forgets what is buried in its bones.

Text Copyright

First Edition

About the Author

Belinda writes layered mysteries where memory lingers, landscapes remember, and silence speaks louder than words. Her stories slip between the literary and the intimate—part atmospheric suspense, part quiet reckoning. Rooted in a love for islands, history, and hidden truths, her work invites readers to linger in the in-between.

She believes some lands carry echoes of everything they've witnessed—grief, joy, betrayal—and that nostalgia for place is its own kind of story. When she's not writing, Belinda tends to her garden, guided by the rustle of leaves, the smell of earth, and the quiet company of two cats who always seem

to know more than they let on.

Table of Contents

Prologue

The ocean was too quiet. That's what bothered him. No gulls, no breeze. Just the slap of water against the hull, slow and thick, like something breathing.

Jean-Michel Larocque wiped sweat from his brow, squinting into the mist. The islet should've been empty—just coral and scrub. But someone had lit a fire. Blue, flickering, wrong.

"This is private land," he said, louder than he meant to. His voice cracked. "You hear me?"

No answer. Just the wind shifting—carrying a smell. Burnt cloves? Sulphur?

He stepped off the boat. Sand gave way under his feet. His chest tightened. A sharp whistle echoed—like a child calling a dog. Then silence.

Behind him, the boat untethered itself.

In front of him, the flame rose.

His scream never made it past his lips.

Chapter 1

I'm Dr. Amaya Zarin—forensic anthropologist, former consultant for the Metropolitan Police, published expert on colonial-era burial misclassifications, unwanted daughter of this island. I left Zaka with a scholarship and a suitcase. I returned with a funeral notice and a bad feeling.

They said my uncle died peacefully.

I wasn't there when they burned him.

The cremation happened without me. A state formality—no rites, no song, no scattered petals. Just bureaucracy and flame. They said it was peaceful.

But peace never smelled like burnt clove and regret.

Uncle Yannis had raised me when my parents went to work in Paris and never fully came back. He taught me how to listen to bones, how to ask questions even when people called them curses. He taught me that the island remembered things we'd buried.

When the neighbour emailed, it didn't say much—just that he was gone. The cause was listed as natural. I've studied death long enough to know "natural" often just means "no one's looking too closely."

His house hadn't changed.

Still full of jars that smelled like time. Still humming with the kind of quiet that felt alive. Still too warm, like it didn't want to let go of whoever left last.

The box sat on the kitchen table.

Wooden. Locked. My name scratched into the top with his old field knife. The wax seal already cracked.

Inside was his journal.

And tucked between the pages—

A photograph of Maïa Saramine with Yannis and me and another one of Maïa alone.

***

She couldn't have been more than seventeen. Jasmine in her hair. Grinning like the island didn't scare her yet. The banyan tree behind her twisted like a memory too stubborn to rot.

Behind the photo, a sketch.

The glyph.

The same one she used to draw in the margins of her notebooks. The same one she traced on my arm once with a stick of sugarcane ash, saying, "It keeps the bad spirits on the outside."

I didn't believe her then.

I wasn't sure what I believed now.

***

I pressed the photo to my chest.

"I'm sorry I left," I whispered.

Chapter 2

Last time I flew in, it was for death. This time, it's for truth. That familiar crescent of green cliffs and red tin rooftops, framed by sea like an offering. From above, Isle de Zaka looked untouched. Pure. Like nothing had ever bled here.

But I knew better.

When Zaka authorities asked if I'd consult and help the police with my acquired expertise in Europe after my visit—I said yes.

Maybe I came for the work.

Maybe I came for Yannis.

Maybe I came for Maïa.

Maybe I came for myself.

So here I am—coming back not for grief, not even for justice. I came back because the past has bones. And I know how to read them.

***

I shifted in my seat and opened the box tucked under my arm. The wood had warped slightly in the London cold, but the clasp still clicked like it remembered me.

Yannis' journal sat inside, wrapped in old muslin.

A note taped to the cover in his slanted scrawl:

"If I'm gone, don't forget what the island won't say out loud."

I hadn't read past the first page since I retrieved it three months ago. It felt wrong to turn the pages when my heart was still cracked open.

But the photo tucked behind the cover still stared at me.

Maïa.

Seventeen.

Hair wild. Laugh too loud. Eyes too bright.

She'd vanished twenty years ago. They said illness. Cremation. No body.

Same story.

Same silence.

Behind the photo was a drawing. A symbol I didn't understand.

***

The seatbelt light flickered. The plane dipped slightly, catching the curve of Zaka's southern edge.

I closed the box.

Pressed the photo tighter between the pages.

And whispered,

"I'm here now."

We landed in Port Princess, the southern armpit of the island—humid, flat, always smelling like jet fuel and overripe mango. I stepped off the plane, and the air hit me like a memory. Salt. Smoke. Sugarcane ash.

Ravi was late.

Of course he was. Inspector Gran Ravi Caderamen always said clocks were "a colonial invention."

Instead, Ti-Kiki showed up.

Kiran Roopramanien, ex-fisherman, part-time rum baron, full-time nuisance. The island called him Ti-Kiki because no one remembers calling him anything else. He had the mouth of a drunk uncle, the eyes of someone who knew where the bodies were buried, and the scent of clove smoke and old rum casks trailing behind him.

He pulled up in a dented pickup with a machete strapped to the dashboard and two pineapples in the passenger seat like they were paying for the ride.

"You smell like plane," he said. "And mainland doubt."

I didn't smile. "You smell like someone who should've picked me up on time."

"Blame the dead guy," he said.

He grinned. "Ravi's busy. We got a fresh dead man on the beach near Bel Zaka."

"How fresh?"

"Still steaming when they found him. Locals say it's Zaka's flame."

"And you?"

"I say he probably pissed off the wrong spirits. Or wife. Or accountant."

He tossed me a cold bottle of Phoenix beer. "Welcome home, Aya."

Chapter 3

The road from Port Princess to Bel Zaka curled like a lazy serpent—too narrow for comfort, too beautiful for panic. We passed rusting billboards for spiritual retreats, cracked sugarcane fields, and roadside shrines so old the gods were barely visible anymore.

Kiki didn't talk for a while. He let the tires hum. Let the silence stretch.

Finally, he said, "You are really going to stay this time?"

I kept my eyes on the window. "Depends how many bodies wash up."

"Still talking like a mainlander."

"Still deflecting like a Zakais."

"Touché."

He offered me a slice of pineapple. I didn't take it.

"You know who the dead man is yet?" I asked.

"Everyone does."

"But no one's saying it out loud?"

"This is Zaka. We don't say names until we're sure they can't hear us back."

He turned off the main road and followed a dirt track toward the beach. The air changed—cooler, quieter. The trees here leaned closer together, like they were whispering behind our backs.

"Jean-Michel Laroque," he said finally.

"The hotel guy?"

"Zaka Essence. The one with the infinity pool and the guilt-free colonial design."

I frowned. "He was expanding, right? Buying protected land?"

Kiki snorted. "Protected on paper. Sacred in practice."

The truck creaked to a stop.

Ahead, just past the treeline, I saw the flash of blue tarpaulin and crime scene tape. The scent hit next—salt, rot, and something sharper underneath. Not blood. Not quite.

Burnt cloves.

***

We stepped out onto the sand. It was still early, but the heat was already rising in waves. A few junior officers milled about near the scene, trying to look official while keeping their distance from the tarp-covered body.

And there he was - Inspector Ravi Caderamen.

Back straight, arms crossed, face carved from the same stone they used for colonial statues. The only thing different about him was the grey in his beard. And the rosary beads tucked into the waistband of his slacks.

He turned as I approached, jaw tightening just a touch. Not quite a smile. Not quite a scowl. Just enough to say: *I'm surprised, but not pleased.*

"Dr. Zarin."

"Inspector."

He looked me over like I was a package that had arrived late and badly labelled.

"You've been gone a long time."

"You've been standing still a long time."

He met my gaze. Steady. Too steady. Like a man still guarding something sacred—or rotten.

He exhaled through his nose. "I didn't ask you to come."

"That makes two of us. The body did."

Behind me, Kiki gave a low whistle and wandered off toward the shoreline. Wise man.

"Jean-Michel Laroque," I said. "That's the official word?"

"As official as it gets around here."

He gestured toward the body with a small nod. "Want to take a look?"

"Always."

We walked toward the tarp.

"Before you open it," he said, "you should know... the heat damage is unusual. For here."

"You mean the sun didn't do it."

"And neither did a match."

He lifted the edge of the tarp.

Even with the humidity, the body was dry. *Too* dry. Charred in patches, but not uniformly. Like the fire had started *inside him,* then *stopped.* The eyes were gone, sockets black and hollow. His hands were curled. The sand beneath him had singed, but not spread.

I crouched beside the body, squinting.

Something glittered in the creases of his burnt skin—fine grains of glass. Fused sand.

"He burned," I said softly. "But not by fire. By heat."

Ravi didn't answer.

Instead, he looked up at the trees.

And for just a second—just one heartbeat—I thought I saw fear in his eyes.

"Zaka's watching," he murmured.

"No," I said. "Zaka's warning."

A throat cleared behind us.

I turned to see a woman—late twenties, sharp posture, clipboard in hand, eyes doing that thing where they flick from the body to me to Ravi to my boots to the trees. She had the air of someone who was trying very hard to look like she wasn't trying at all.

"Sorry to interrupt, Inspector. We bagged the fibres from the shoreline. Nothing synthetic."

She shifted her attention to me, and I saw it: recognition. Curiosity. A flicker of intimidation she tried to blink away.

"You must be Dr. Zarin."

"And you are?"

"Officer Savita Naidee. Everyone calls me Ti-Sav."

She stuck out her hand like she meant it.

I shook it. Firm grip. Warm palms.

She smelled like sunscreen and mosquito repellent. Field girl.

"You trained in South Africa?" I asked.

She blinked, surprised. "Stellenbosch. How'd you—"

"Boots. Gait. And you muttered 'fire doesn't climb sideways' in Afrikaans when you saw the burn patterns."

She flushed, then grinned. "I've read your work. On the British excavation errors in Bengal. That paper pissed a lot of people off."

"Good. That means they read it."

Behind us, Ravi cleared his throat—not gently.

"We don't have time for academic courtship. There's a body here. A man with enemies. And a hotel full of lawyers on speed dial."

"And no witnesses," Ti-Sav added, glancing around. "Except maybe..."

She pointed up.

In the trees above, a row of woven talismans dangled from a line. Bones, feathers, bits of glass tied with twine. One had cracked in half.

"Local protection charms," she said. "Hung up last week, apparently. And now one's broken."

She hesitated, voice lower now. "They say when one breaks, it means a spirit's been let out."

"They?" I asked.

She shrugged. "My grandmother. Most of the village. Probably Kiki, too, if he wasn't busy smoking sea air."

"Do you believe it?"

"I believe it's never broken before. Until today."

I looked at Ravi. He didn't say anything.

But he didn't roll his eyes either.

Chapter 4

I crouched again beside the body. The heat damage was bizarre—uneven, internal, like a blast furnace had kissed him from the inside. His fingers were curled like he'd clutched something before death. I reached for my kit.

"May I?" I asked.

Ravi gave the faintest nod.

"It's your scene now, apparently."

Ti-Sav handed me a pair of gloves. Bless her. Already anticipating my next move.

I slid them on and began the process: slow, meticulous. The sand beneath him had fused in patches—tiny fragments of vitrified glass where normal sand should be. The burns weren't superficial. They came from inside his core.

"This isn't combustion," I muttered.

"What is it then?" Ti-Sav asked.

"Thermal destabilization. Something cooked him. Not from fire. From..."

I hesitated.

"...pressure. Heat. Intensity. Like lightning. Or worse."

I peeled back his shirt—what was left of it. The skin underneath was blackened, but not in the usual pattern of flame damage. More like...

"It moved with him," I whispered. "It followed his veins."

"That's not science," Ravi grunted.

"No. But it's what the body says."

We catalogued everything. Jewellery (burnt). No phone. Watch melted. A faint smell of cloves and metal, unnatural and lingering. Nearby, I spotted a charred offering bowl, half-sunken into the sand.

"Zaka offering?" I asked.

Ti-Sav nodded. "Could be. Or someone faked one. Tourists buy them all the time from the markets."

"What would a hotel owner be doing with one out here?"

"Appeasing. Or provoking."

"Either way," I said, "he failed."

***

I turned from the body, letting the image burn into memory like heat does metal.

And that's when I saw it.

Not on the body.

Not carved into skin like ritual.

But marked—carefully—on the stone just beyond the tide line. Half-covered by sand. Dark, almost like burned ink.

A spiral.

Split at the centre, like something cleaved.

One half shaded; one left bare.

Beneath it, a root-like symbol. Veins? Coral? I couldn't tell.

And just beneath that—three dots. Like a triangle. Or a countdown.

"What is that?" I asked.

Ravi turned. His face didn't move.

"They're calling it a symbol. Maybe a warning. No one's touched it yet."

I crouched down, pulse ticking louder.

My fingers itched to draw it.

But my mind already had.

I'd seen it before.

Long ago. In Maïa's notebook.

And again, just yesterday, behind a photo in a dead man's journal.

* * *

Samples was bagged, the scene cleared and the body removed an hour later.

The sun was hotter now. The kind of heat that made metal sing and trees crack open. We were headed back to the road when Ravi finally broke his silence.

"You sure you're ready to see the hotel?"

"Why wouldn't I be?"

"Because this place, Dr. Zarin, is not built for people who ask too many questions."

* * *

By the time we reached Zaka Essence, the air felt heavier. Not hot—dense, like sound moved slower here.

The main building gleamed—white stone walls wrapped in vines, open-air corridors with linen curtains drifting lazily in the salt wind. A place built to make you forget the world. Or hide from it.

"He really called it Zaka Essence?" I muttered.

Ravi gave a grunt that might've been a laugh. Or gas.

"He said it honoured the island's spirit."

"Zaka doesn't need a spa menu and minibar."

"Try telling that to the guests."

The receptionist gave us the kind of tight, professional smile you use at funerals and tax audits.

"Ah, Inspector. You're early."

"We're not. The body was."

She winced.

"If you'll follow me, our head of staff is waiting."

As we followed her through the halls, I scanned everything. Polished floors. Incense burning. A statue of Zaka carved in faux-obsidian—wearing an absurd golden robe. I rolled my eyes.

"This place is a shrine to appropriation," I said.

"It's a business," Ravi said flatly. "And it brings in tourist money."

"So does selling fake gris-gris charms in the market. Doesn't mean it's sacred."

We passed through the healing garden—lavender, lemongrass, and a carved banyan stump in the centre. Someone had left half-burned cloves and a cracked egg in the dirt.

"Guests?" I asked.

Ravi shook his head. "Staff don't talk. Not yet."

We reached the staff office, a quiet little room behind the yoga studio. Inside: Anita Dambreville, hotel manager, mid-40s, tight bun, tighter mouth. She stood when we entered but didn't offer a smile.

"You're here about Jean-Michel?" she asked.

"You mean the man found charred on a public beach?" I replied.

"I mean the owner of this hotel. And my employer. Until this morning."

"When did you last see him?"

"Two nights ago. He was at dinner with the—"

She hesitated.

"—the healer. I didn't disturb them."

Ravi looked at me.

I looked back.

The healer. Of course.

"Where is this healer now?" I asked.

Anita pressed her lips together. "Still on-site. Guests insist. They... trust her."

"Do you?"

"I don't trust anyone who won't sleep in their own room."

***

The healer stayed in a stone bungalow just off the healing garden—separate from the guest suites, tucked behind a curtain of palm fronds and frangipani trees. The kind of place where incense never stops burning and every shadow feels *intentional*.

Ravi walked beside me, tight-lipped.

"You'll let me speak?" I asked.

"You can speak," he said. "Just don't promise her anything. Or accuse her. Or let her bless you. Or curse you."

"You sound nervous, Inspector."

"I'm not nervous."

"Then why do you smell like cloves?"

"Because I carry them. Like everyone else who's not stupid."

He knocked once.

The door opened without a sound.

She stood in the doorway like she'd *been waiting*.

***

The Healer was Malini Sèvère. Early 40s, maybe younger, maybe older. Her skin the colour of midnight tea and she was wearing long silver earrings and a dark wrap dress that moved like mist. Her voice was smooth, accented, neither entirely Creole nor Bhojpuri—*something older*. Her eyes? Too steady. Too quiet. Like the sea before a cyclone.

"You must be the bone reader," she said to me. Not a question.

I raised an eyebrow. "And you must be the woman dining with a dead man the night before he cooked from the inside out."

"He was already burning," she said softly. "Long before that night."

***

The inside of her bungalow was half apothecary, half altar. There were shelves of dried herbs, oils, ashes, cloth bundles. At the centre was a wooden table carved with symbols Amaya almost—but not quite—recognized. In the corner was a bowl still steaming with cloves, cinnamon bark, something black and slick that looked suspiciously like bloodroot in it.

Ravi shifted behind me. Arms crossed. His discomfort practically *screamed.*

"Tell us about the dinner," I said.

Malini smiled. It was not a comforting smile.

"He asked about cleansing."

"Of what?"

"Land. Guilt. The feeling that something was... following him."

"Was it?"

She looked directly at me.

"We all have something following us."

***

"Did you give him anything?" Ravi asked.

"I offered protection."

"A charm?"

"A warning."

She crossed the room and pulled open a small drawer. From inside, she withdrew a piece of scorched palm parchment, etched in black ink. A spell. A prayer. A diagram.

"He burned it," she said. "He said it felt too real."

***

"And what is it?" I asked.

"A glyph to keep out things that listen."

Her gaze didn't leave mine.

"But you already know about those, don't you, Dr. Zarin?"

***

I stepped closer to the glyph. It shimmered faintly—like the ink hadn't dried, even though it clearly had. A circle. A split eye. Something that looked like a root system or veins.

"Where did you learn to write this?" I asked.

"You don't learn. You remember."

"That's poetic. Not helpful."

"Then perhaps you're asking the wrong question."

I turned back to face her.

"Fine. What were you doing on the night Jean-Michel died?"

"Breathing."

"Alone?"

"I'm never alone."

Ravi made a sound behind me—frustrated, almost amused. He was letting me lead, but barely. This wasn't his terrain. Malini made him itch.

"Did you see him after dinner?" I pressed.

"He came back. Just before midnight."

"Why?"

"To ask if the flame was real."

"And you told him?"

"That it doesn't care what we believe. Only what we disturb."

I stepped even closer. She didn't move. Didn't flinch.

"He disturbed something, didn't he?"

"He tried to own something that could not be owned."

"Land?"

"Spirit."

"And you warned him?"

"Yes."

"What did he say?"

She paused. And finally—finally—her voice changed. Softer. Tired.

"He said... 'Zaka is a legend. Fear is good business. And you, Malini, are just part of the show.'"

***

She set the glyph down gently.

"So, I told him," She said, "if he wanted to burn the offering, he should do it under the banyan tree. Where the spirits wouldn't miss it."

"And did he?"

"The wind that night shifted east. Toward the sea. Toward the Flame."

***

I studied her.

The performance had cracks now. Behind the calm was something deeper—regret, maybe. Or worse... satisfaction.

"You didn't stop him," I said.

"I lit the incense," she replied. "And I prayed it would be enough."

"Enough for what?"

"For the island to leave him alone."

She met my eyes, finally letting something *move* behind hers.

"But you know, don't you, Dr. Zarin?"

"Know what?"

"Once the island knows your name... it never forgets your breath."

Chapter 5

Ravi pulled me out of there with a muttered curse and a visible shiver.

As we stepped back into the sun, he said, "We're not charging her. Not yet. But she's involved."

"She didn't kill him," I said.

"You sound sure."

"She didn't need to."

***

The path to Villa Fire wound past the edge of the healing garden and dipped into a thin patch of wild cane and twisted palms. The deeper we went, the more the resort faded behind us—less yoga, more silence. Not the peaceful kind. The kind that waits.

The villa stood alone, perched over the sea on black volcanic rock. From a distance, it looked untouched. Up close? The details told a different story.

The wooden door was warped. The metal handle scorched. The air smelled faintly of *charred salt and cloves.*

Ravi unlocked it with a key Anita had given him, reluctantly.

"She said the staff refuse to come here now," he muttered.

"Smart staff."

The door creaked open.

***

The inside of Villa Fire was open-plan with its main room minimalist, and luxurious in a curated, colonial-chic way. The furniture was in teak with silk cushions. A massive glass wall overlooks the ocean. In the centre of the room was a circle of scorched floorboards, blackened in a perfect radius—like a ritual had taken place... or something had *erupted*.

"What did the forensics team say?" I asked.

"They didn't. They refused to go in."

I crouched near the blackened wood. No ash. No soot. Just clean, burned geometry. That was unnatural. Fire always left chaos. This was... purposeful.

Ti-Sav's voice came over Ravi's walkie.

"Sir, no prints on the patio. But the security feed was cut at 11:17 p.m. Camera's intact, wire's clean."

"Surgically cut," I muttered. "Planned. Someone wanted this space invisible."

＊

I moved toward the bedside drawer and found books, receipts, incense sticks and matches inside. Boring. The second drawer was locked.

Ravi handed me his multi-tool without a word.

Click.

Inside the second drawer was a handwritten journal with a cracked leather cover, a sealed envelope labelled *"For her. If she comes back"*. Also, in it was a photo of a young woman—me—on the island, age seventeen, standing beside a banyan tree I hadn't seen in years

"He knew," I whispered.

Ravi looked over my shoulder. "Knew what?"

"That I'd come back."

"Why?"

"Because something was unfinished. And he knew where it started."

I opened the journal.

On the first page was a symbol.

The same glyph Malini had shown me.

Only older. Rougher. Etched in faded ink that curled at the edges like it had resisted the page.

***

I held the photo in one hand, the journal in the other.

Seventeen. That was me. Hair longer. Face younger. That banyan tree behind me—the one near Saint-Amour, the one Grandmère said was "where the earth listens."

I hadn't even known this photo existed.

"He had this," I said softly. "All this time."

"Did you give it to him?" Ravi asked.

I shook my head. "No. And that's not the strange part."

"What is?"

I turned the photo over. One line, written in that same tight, slanted script I hadn't seen since before he died:

"Zaka chooses the ones who remember."

***

I tucked the photo into my coat. Took the journal. Closed the drawer slowly—like whatever was inside might still be watching.

"Let's go," I said.

Ravi didn't argue.

As we left, I turned back—just once. The wind kicked up, stirring the ashes in that perfect circle. And for half a second, I swore I saw the burn line pulse.

Just once.

Like something breathing.

Chapter 6

I was seventeen when I first saw the glyph.

It wasn't in a book. Not in a dream. Not in some colonial archive under fluorescent lights.

It was carved into the skin of a banyan tree behind my grandmother's house—where the vines hung like veils and the wind carried secrets.

Where even the birds stopped singing after dark.

***

The day was hot. Muggy. Zaka's Eve, the last full moon before cyclone season. The island felt like it was holding its breath.

I was barefoot, half-mad with the ache of leaving. I had a scholarship. A flight. A new name to build for myself in a place that didn't believe in ghosts.

But that morning, Grandmère looked at me and said:

"You don't leave the island clean, Amaya. You only carry what hasn't followed you yet."

***

She sent me to gather herbs—basil, lime leaf, ash bark. I took the back trail through the forest. The long one. The one I wasn't supposed to walk alone.

That's when I saw them.

A group of elders I didn't recognize—hooded, still, circled around the banyan. In the centre: a small fire, burning blue.

One by one, they traced the glyph in ash on the ground, then cut their palms and let blood drip into the roots.

I didn't move. I barely breathed.

But one of them turned. Looked straight at me.

He didn't speak.

He just raised his hand, and pointed behind me—to the sea.

***

I ran.

I told no one.

Not even my grandmother.

But that night, while packing, I found a folded paper tucked into my bag.

A sketch of the glyph.

And a note in my uncle's handwriting:

"We don't choose to remember. We're chosen."

***

Years passed.

Science replaced ritual. Data replaced fear.

But the glyph stayed with me—in dreams, in scars, in the way I flinched when the wind changed direction.

And now it was back.

On a corpse.

In a villa.

Tied to a man who once called belief "a product for spiritual tourists."

***

I opened the journal.

Turned to the first page with shaking fingers.

Beneath the glyph were four words, underlined once.

"Zaka remembers your blood."

Chapter 7

By the time I got back to the forensics station near Port Lumière, it was already late afternoon. The sun was beginning to dip, throwing gold across the bay, like the island was pretending nothing ever burned.

Inside the low concrete building, the AC barely worked. The fridge buzzed louder than the computers. A crucifix hung sideways on the wall above the coffee maker.

And Ti-Sav was there—lounging on the edge of a cluttered desk, sipping mango juice like she owned the place.

"You're back," she said.

"You're lounging."

"I lounge best when people bring me things to analyse."

I tossed the journal on the table.

She blinked. "This isn't a 'thing.' This is a *vibe*."

***

She opened it, carefully, reverently. Flipped past the first few pages.

"Is this... your uncle's?"

"Apparently. Found it in Villa Fire."

"This looks like field notes mixed with prophecy."

"That's Zaka in a nutshell."

***

She flipped to the glyph. Her fingers paused on the edges.

"I've seen this before," she whispered.

I looked up.

"Where?"

"The old archives at the National Museum. In a sealed exhibit on the Riots of 1871. Someone carved it into the walls of a burned-out sugar mill. They called it 'marking the island for vengeance.'"

"Was it documented?"

"Nope. Removed. Quietly. Too many tourists didn't like the word 'vengeance' near the snack bar."

***

I took a breath. The room felt smaller.

"Ti-Sav... I need your help. I don't need a sidekick. I need a partner."

Her eyes lit up. "I knew you'd say that eventually."

"Don't make it weird."

"I'm *going* to make it weird."

***

"Does Ravi know?" she asked.

"Not yet."

"Good. He'd make you file a report before he let you follow your own bloodline."

She closed the book, gently.

"So, what now?"

"Now we find out what Laroque was doing with that glyph. And why he thought it would protect him."

"You think it was protection?"

I looked at her.

"I think it was *bait*."

***

Ti-Sav cleared the whiteboard of outdated case notes, then started sketching out names with a purple marker like she was designing a conspiracy theory podcast cover.

I leaned against the desk, arms crossed, watching her work.

"This isn't evidence," I said.

"It's intuition," she replied. "It's Zaka."

"Let's try to keep at least *half* the board admissible in court."

"Fine. But if something starts bleeding when I write it down, that's *your* problem."

***

Anita Dambreville – Hotel Manager

- Controlled. Cold. Knows more than she says.

- Last person to *officially* see Laroque before dinner with Malini

- Motive? Possibly angry about the hotel expansion risking her position

- Hidden agenda: seems too calm about her boss being roasted like coconut

Malini Sèvère – Resident Healer

- Said Laroque was "already burning"

- Gave him a glyph she *knew* was dangerous

- Motive? Protecting sacred land / punishing a violator

- Hidden detail: never said she saw him die, but her words danced awfully close to it

Rohan Beedassy – Bartender (not yet introduced)

- Supposedly off-duty that night... but there's a back entrance to the villa bar
- Knows all the guest gossip
- Possible link to black-market charm sales (???)

The Guests (VIP Suite Zone)

- 3 couples + 1 solo guest on record
- But Malini claims there were seven people at dinner
- Who's not listed? Who left before police arrived?

✳✳✳

Ti-Sav stepped back and capped the marker.

"There's always someone missing from the list," she said.

"Always someone no one wants to name."

I nodded. "We find that person... we find the flame."

Chapter 8

Zaka Essence looked different at dusk.

The sunlight had softened, the shadows lengthened, and the healing garden buzzed with the hush of wind and incense and guilt. Guests were drifting toward the Flame Bar—the resort's open-air lounge suspended over the cliff edge like it had no intention of ever falling.

That's where we found Rohan Beedassy, the bartender. He was late 30s, lean, sharp-cheeked, with a messy ponytail and tired eyes that missed nothing. He had one sleeve of tattoos—part Hindu iconography, part compass roses and smelled like clove cigarettes and sugarcane. His voice was like molasses and his humour like a scalpel.

He saw us coming and was already halfway through polishing a glass he didn't need to polish.

"If it isn't the mainland hurricane and the girl with the clipboard," he said.

"You weren't supposed to be here today," Ravi said.

"I'm always here. Even when I'm not."

"You were listed as off-duty the night Laroque died."

"I was. Doesn't mean I was absent."

He poured three glasses of water. Didn't ask if we wanted anything stronger.

***

"Where were you?" I asked.

"Behind the bar."

"No one saw you."

"That's the point of being behind the bar."

He gestured toward the glowing liquor shelf—lit with low amber light like a shrine to secrets.

"Jean-Michel came through just after ten. Two glasses of Grand Bay Rum. Took them with him."

"To the villa?"

"Not directly. He stopped to speak with Malini. Then he left alone."

"Anyone with him earlier?"

"Anita came by around eight. They argued. Quietly. But I notice quiet arguments more than loud ones. They linger longer."

***

Ti-Sav took notes. I watched his hands.

Calm. Unflinching.

"Did you see anything strange?" I asked.

"Strange is this hotel's business model."

"Anything *newly* strange?"

He paused. Thought. Then leaned forward just slightly.

"He started walking barefoot," Rohan said. "Even at night. Said he needed to feel the island under him. Said 'the shoes make it harder to hear.'"

***

Silence fell between us.

Even Ravi didn't have a comeback for that.

***

"One more thing," I said.

"Did he ever mention the Cave of Embers?"

Rohan's smile thinned.

"He went once. Months ago. Came back quieter. Asked for clove tea, not alcohol. I asked what he saw."

"And?"

"He said, '*The flame isn't gone. It's just waiting for someone worth burning.*'"

***

Ravi exhaled through his nose.

"We're going to need to talk to Anita again."

"You think she's hiding something?" Ti-Sav asked.

"I think everyone here is," I said.

"Including you?" Rohan added smoothly.

I met his eyes. Didn't blink.

"Especially me."

***

Ravi said nothing as we walked back through the lobby.

He didn't need to.

I could feel him watching me again—not as a partner, not even as a sceptic.

As a man waiting to see how far I was willing to go before I cracked something open we couldn't put back.

Anita Dambreville was back at her desk, surrounded by perfect order. A glass of still water. A stack of updated invoices. Her fingers didn't stop moving even as we approached.

"Rohan's memory seems very intact," I said.

"Does it?" she replied, not looking up.

"You didn't mention that you and Jean-Michel argued the night he died."

"I didn't think it was relevant. We argued often. It was part of the creative process."

"Sounds like therapy."

"Sounds like hospitality."

***

Ravi stepped forward—just a hair.

Enough to remind us *who wore the badge.*

"Did he mention the glyph? The spiritual symbols?"

"He was obsessed with them. Said the 'Zaka brand' needed more authenticity. He wanted the healer to do rituals for VIP guests. Stage them, of course."

"And you?"

"I thought it was insulting. And dangerous. You don't play with gods just to get better reviews."

Her eyes flicked to mine.

"Especially not gods who remember when you stopped believing."

***

Before I could ask more, a voice behind us cut in—smooth, bright, and half-drunk.

"Is this where I'm supposed to report a murder? Or is there a form for that?"

We turned.

Tall. Early 50s. Tan skin, expensive linen, smug smile. Luc Garnier introduced himself as a French national and repeat visitor to Zaka Essence claimed that he was a "spiritual art collector" which we should read as rich man with a guilt complex and a shrine to himself. He was arrogant, charming, shady and not on the guest list for dinner... but may have been watching from the shadows.

"I saw Jean-Michel the night he died," Luc said casually. "From the balcony. He was barefoot. Speaking to the banyan tree."

"What was he saying?" I asked.

"Hard to hear. But he poured rum into the soil and said something like, *If this is your land, take it.*"

I blinked.

"And then?"

"He walked toward the cliff. Alone. I assumed he was going to think about bad investments."

"You didn't think to mention this to the police?" Ravi asked, voice sharp.

Luc sipped his cocktail.

"You didn't ask."

Chapter 9

The whiteboard was now a riot of scribbles, arrows, and circled names. It looked like madness. It *was* madness. But it was starting to hum with pattern.

Ti-Sav clicked her pen like a metronome.

***

TIMELINE: THE NIGHT OF LAROQUE'S DEATH

7:00 PM – Dinner service begins.

8:00 PM – Anita seen arguing with Laroque. Leaves.

8:30 PM – Laroque drinks with Malini in the garden.

10:00 PM – Rohan says Laroque takes two rums, goes barefoot.

11:00 PM – Seen speaking to banyan tree by Luc Garnier.

11:17 PM – Security feed cuts.

By sunrise – Found dead on public beach, scorched from the inside.

***

CURRENT SUSPECTS:

Anita Dambreville

- Motive: Job loss, resentment
- Behaviour: Controlled, secretive
- Gaps: Her alibi stops at 9 PM

Malini Sèvère

- Motive: Sacred land protector?

- Involvement: Gave Laroque the glyph

- Wildcard: Knows something she won't say

Rohan Beedassy

- Motive: Unknown (yet)

- Knows more than he admits

- Connection to glyphs?

Luc Garnier

- "Wasn't at dinner"—but saw everything

- Creepy calm. Could be lying.

- Possible connection to Laroque's investments?

***

"It's not about who hated him," Ti-Sav said. "It's about who *knew* what he touched."

I nodded. "And what touched back."

* * *

Back in her grandmother's house, Amaya sat alone later that night. The journal is opened in her lap. A storm was brewing outside—the kind that always comes after Zaka's name is spoken too often.

* * *

She flips to a page half-stuck together. Peels it open carefully.

ENTRY – March 18

"He found it. The root flame. Said he felt it under his skin. I told him to stop digging. He said the land wanted to be opened."

"I heard something last night. By the banyan. Not the wind. A breath. A whisper."

"If she ever returns, tell her not to follow this trail. Tell her it doesn't end where she thinks."

And beneath that:

A sketch of a map.

With three sacred sites marked.

One of them circled in red ink:

"Cave of Embers – final site"

✳✳✳

Cicadas screamed outside.

At a small, smoke-stained bar off the coast road that same night.

Ravi sat across from Mervin Soopayah, his old mentor—retired, mostly deaf, fully sharp.

"You let her in," Soopayah said. "The Zarin girl."

"I didn't let her," Ravi muttered. "I just didn't stop her."

"Same thing."

"She's good."

"She's dangerous."

Ravi sipped his drink. Didn't answer.

Soopayah tapped a folder on the table. Unmarked. Old.

Inside were newspaper clippings, photos and a list of names crossed out in pencil.

"That fire in '87 near Saint-Amour," the old man said. "The one they blamed on smugglers. That wasn't smuggling."

Ravi stared. "What was it then?"

"The last time someone tried to wake Zaka."

Chapter 10

The call came in just after midnight.

Ti-Sav's phone buzzed first. She was already half-asleep on the couch at the station, marker ink still on her fingers from the board.

"You need to see this," said the voice on the other end. "Now."

***

By 1:00 AM, we were at the northern docks near Port Royal.

Fishing boats bobbed under dull sodium lights. Police tape fluttered in the salt wind. A small crowd had already gathered, murmuring in low Creole—crosses drawn on chests, amulets clutched in fists.

Ravi was already there, jaw locked, hands in his coat pockets.

"Who is it?" I asked.

"Luc Garnier," he said.

"Dead?"

"Dead doesn't cover it."

***

They found him on the wooden jetty, body twisted unnaturally, eyes gone, mouth wide open like he'd tried to scream the truth and failed.

Burn marks laced his chest—not random. A symbol. A glyph.

This time, not drawn. Not tattooed.

Branded.

Into the skin.

Still smouldering.

✳✳✳

"He said that he saw Laroque walking barefoot," I muttered.

"Maybe now he saw too much," Ravi said grimly.

Ravi flipped his notebook closed slowly, eyes lingering just a second too long. He didn't need to ask what came next. He already knew.

Ti-Sav's voice wavered. "What does it mean? That the glyph moved?"

"No," I said. "It chose again."

I crouched beside the body. His hand was clenched tight.

Inside, folded like a message: a single strip of parchment.

Scorched at the edges.

Written in the same hand as the journal.

"The fire is not revenge. It is memory."

Chapter 11

I hadn't slept.

The lab was quiet—just the soft hum of the fridge, the rhythmic click of Ti-Sav typing in the next room, and the tick of my gloved fingers brushing across charred fibres beneath the microscope.

Luc Garnier's body had burned from the inside out. Just like Laroque.

But something had changed. The branding.

More than rage. More than message.

It was signature.

And signatures came from people who *wanted to be remembered.*

***

I flipped to a fresh page in my notes and wrote:

Active characteristics:

– Control

– Ritual consistency

– Message delivery

– No physical struggle

– Post-mortem placement (the body wasn't dumped—it was *displayed*)

Likely:

– Charismatic

– Mission-driven

– Possibly delusional

– Deep familiarity with island history and sacred sites

– Likely male (though not necessarily)

– Age: Unknown, but physically capable

– Education level: High

I paused. Underlined "Message delivery" three times.

"This isn't revenge," I whispered. "It's performance."

***

I moved to the samples.

Garnier's burned palm held parchment. Ancient-looking, but recent. Ashes flaked from the edges.

I ran a solvent test. Traces of iron oxide. Charcoal. Cinnamon oil.

A mix consistent with ritual ink—used in Bhojpuri protection spells.

Not decorative.

Deliberate.

The killer was mimicking sacred symbols, but warping them—*perverting belief into punishment.*

***

Footsteps behind me.

Ti-Sav leaned in the doorway with a cup of cold coffee and worry all over her face.

"Any leads?" she asked.

"Yes," I said.

"Good."

"It's someone who knows how to kill without lifting a finger."

"...Still good?"

"No. Not good at all."

***

We gathered in the briefing room of the Port Lumière station. The fan clacked like it was dying. The projector made the glyph on the wall *glow*.

Ravi, arms folded.

Ti-Sav, typing fast.

Kiki, leaning in the doorway pretending not to listen.

"Walk us through it," Ravi said.

"But keep it grounded."

I stepped forward and clicked to the first slide of the profile of the unidentified suspect.

"Two murders. One week apart. Same pattern. Same symbol—modified. Same internal burning. No external accelerant. No physical evidence of struggle."

"This is not spontaneous violence. It's ritualized execution."

***

I moved to the next slide about my analysis of the psychological markers of the suspect:

- High control;

- Likely male, 30–50;

- Deep cultural knowledge—folklore, sacred site history, spiritual codes;

- Operates with confidence—leaves messages as a signature;

- Feels entitled to deliver punishment; and

- Sees self as a purifier or spiritual messenger.

***

Ravi raised an eyebrow.

"You're saying this is religious?"

"No. I'm saying it's performative belief. Maybe faith. Maybe vengeance. Maybe legacy."

***

Finally, I moved to the last slide of the connecting points:

1. Both victims visited sacred sites—including or near the Cave of Embers;

2. Both interacted with Malini Sèvère shortly before death; and

3. Both left symbolic offerings—not for Zaka, but possibly to appease *someone* using *Zaka's name.*

***

"So, this is what?" Kiki asked. "A killer priest with a poetry degree?"

"Maybe. Or someone who believes we've forgotten something we were supposed to protect."

***

Ravi leaned back, eyes on the wall.

"And where does this lead?"

I clicked the final slide: A map from the journal, with three points glowing like embers.

"It leads to three sites."

"You think these are murder sites?"

"I think they're ritual stages. And we've only seen Act One."

***

Silence. The glyph glowed. The fan clicked.

Finally, Ravi spoke.

"And if you're wrong?"

I didn't blink.

"Then we'll bury a third body."

Chapter 12

The station was nearly empty by the time I found her alone—back in the evidence room, the journal open like it was some kind of holy book, or a bomb.

She didn't look up when I walked in.

"You need to stop treating this case like a legend," I said.

Amaya didn't move. "It became a legend because no one ever solved it."

"You're not here to rewrite Zaka's mythology."

"I'm not. I'm here because people are dying."

***

She finally looked at me.

"You asked me to help. I'm helping."

"No," I said. "I asked you to consult. What you're doing now? You're digging up things the island *buried for a reason.*"

I stepped closer. She didn't flinch—but her fingers clenched tighter around the journal.

"You're not listening to the evidence," she said.

"I'm listening to what's *not* being said. That's what kept me alive here for 20 years."

What he didn't say: silence had kept him safe, but not clean.

"And how many people stayed dead because you listened too quietly?"

***

That hit harder than it should have.

I walked past her, looked down at the map she'd traced from the journal.

The red-circled site: a coastal cave just outside Saint-Amour.

A place I hadn't stepped foot in since before the fire.

"You want to go there?" I spoke.

"Yes."

"Fine."

I looked at her then. Not as a cop. Not even as an islander.

"But if you wake something... you put it back down."

Chapter 13

We hiked down just after dawn, while the sun was still too shy to burn away the salt mist clinging to the cliffs.

The path wasn't marked on any resort maps.

Ti-Sav found it by accident—half-visible on a weathered survey sketch folded into my uncle's journal.

Ravi said nothing the whole way down. Just followed, slow and careful, eyes on everything except us.

The cave waited.

***

They called it "*Trou Lalin*"—Moon Hole.

Once used for offerings to Zaka during the lunar cycle, then abandoned after a child went missing in the 1980s.

Official story: she fell.

Unofficial story: the cave *took her back*.

***

The entrance was wide, wind-carved, and rimmed with black stone. Inside, it narrowed—walls slick with condensation and salt.

No birds. No echo.

Just breath.

And shadows.

***

"Why would your uncle mark this?" Ti-Sav whispered.

"Because this was the *first site*," I said. "Before the Flame. Before the glyph spread."

"And you think the killer came here?"

"No," I said.

"I think they never left."

***

We moved deeper.

The glyph was there—carved into the wall at shoulder height. Fainter than the others. Older. But real.

And beneath it... a pile of broken ceramic.

I knelt.

"Offering bowl," I murmured.

"Like the one near Laroque's body?"

"Not like." I held up a fragment. "*This exact glaze.* Same artisan. Same age."

But there was something else.

✳✳✳

Buried beneath the shards, a fabric. I unwrapped the fabric slowly—old sari cloth, sun-bleached and brittle as leaves.

Inside was a small, dull-gold locket. Burnished. Faint scorch mark on one side. I pried it open with a fingernail.

Just a name inside.

Maïa.

I frowned.

It wasn't uncommon. There must have been a dozen Maïas on the island when I was a child.

But beneath the name, carved into the metal with deliberate, looping precision, was a lotus flower.

Not just any lotus.

One petal curled under, like it was hiding. Like it was shy.

My stomach dropped.

"No," I whispered.

Because Maïa drew that lotus in every one of her school notebooks. On her pencil case. On the inside of her ankle in ballpoint pen when she was nervous.

It was her signature.

Her spell.

Her way of staying grounded.

***

Ti-Sav crouched beside me. "What is it?"

"This symbol... I haven't seen it in twenty years."

"Whose was it?"

"...A girl I went to school with."

"And?"

"And she's dead."

I stared at the locket.

"She has to be."

***

But she wasn't.

Because no one buries a locket twenty years after a funeral.

Not unless they want it to be found.

***

The cave exhaled around us.

I wasn't sure if the cold I felt was from the air, or from the past trying to crawl back up through the cracks.

Chapter 14

Ravi was back at the station when we returned from the cave, seated at his desk like he hadn't moved—like he'd *been waiting.*

The locket was in my pocket, warm from the heat of my palm. I hadn't let go of it since I found it.

"We need to talk," I said.

He didn't look up. "About the glyph?"

"No."

I pulled the locket from my pocket and set it on his desk.

"About Maïa."

***

The moment the name left my mouth, I saw it.

The shift.

The flicker.

The memory behind his eyes.

He didn't ask *which* Maïa.

Because he already knew.

***

"That was a long time ago," he said.

"And?"

"She died."

"We never saw the body."

"There was a fire. You remember the fire."

"I remember a *funeral* without a coffin. I remember jasmine and smoke and a grave filled with ash and silence."

"Because that's all there was left."

***

I stared at him. Waiting.

"What aren't you telling me, Ravi?"

***

He looked tired suddenly. Older. As if the name had pulled the years out of him like a tide.

"It wasn't my case. I was new on the force. They told me not to ask questions. Told me she ran. Got involved with someone dangerous. Or worse."

"And you believed that?"

"No."

"Then why didn't you say anything?"

"Because the island wanted her gone."

***

Silence.

I reached into my pocket again. Pulled out the locket. Turned it toward him.

"She left this behind in a cave with Zaka's mark.

After twenty years. Someone wanted it found."

"That doesn't mean she's alive."

"It doesn't mean she's dead either."

***

I walked to the door.

Before I stepped out, I turned.

"You asked me to stop treating this like a legend."

"It's not."

"It's a ghost story."

Chapter 15

We weren't supposed to go past the fence.

That was the rule.

But Maïa didn't care about rules.

She said the land didn't follow them, so why should we?

***

We were both seventeen.

Same school. Different worlds.

Me: scholarship girl. Logic brain. Always pretending I wasn't afraid of the dark.

Her: all mystery and moonlight. Hair like a storm. Eyes that looked through people instead of at them.

"You don't belong here," she told me once.

"Here" meant Zaka.

"Neither do you," I replied.

She smiled. "That's why we find each other."

***

The secret started with a dare.

One Friday after exams, Maïa took me to the edge of the Saint-Amour Forest. Past the banyan tree. Past the fallen shrine. To a hill with cracked stone and no birds.

"This is where they buried the stories," she said.

"The ones that scared the priests."

She dug with her hands.

What we found wasn't bones.

It was a box. Tin. Sealed.

Inside was an old map of sacred sites, a circle symbol—that was the first time I ever saw the glyph, and a note, water-stained but still legible:

"Only those with fire in their blood should seek the breath of Zaka.

The rest will burn."

***

Maïa touched the glyph. Didn't flinch. Said she'd seen it before.

I told her to bury it again.

She said she couldn't.

That night, we made a pact.

"If anything happens," she said,

"you remember this place.

You remember me.

Even if they try to burn me out of your head."

***

I did.

And they did.

And now, twenty years later, she was *back*.

Chapter 16

Zaka didn't keep good records.

It kept stories.

But stories were slippery things—twisted by fear, reshaped by shame. So, I went looking for something harder. Something with a date stamp.

***

My first stop was the old police records archive in Port Princess. The office there smelled like mildew and distrust. A faded poster on the wall read *"Transparency is the First Step to Justice."* It was peeling.

Ti-Sav had called ahead. We had twenty minutes before someone noticed we were looking into a case that was officially closed.

Disappearance File – Maïa R. Saran

Date: March 24, 20 years ago

Status: Presumed Dead

Body: Not Recovered

Cause: "Likely accident or animal-related incident. No signs of foul play."

I flipped the page.

The signature on the final report wasn't Ravi's. But the handwriting was familiar.

My uncle.

He'd signed off on it.

Even back then... he'd been involved.

***

I went next to the school records in the Sainte-Marie Girls' School. Maïa's grades stopped after Term 1 of that year. No graduation. No transfer.

But one odd thing.

A teacher's note in the margin of her final report card:

"Disruptive. Obsessed with superstitions. Spoke of 'seeing spirits in the forest'—recommend psychological evaluation."

She'd been marked as unstable.

Easy to erase.

Convenient to forget.

****

Finally, I went to my grandmother's house. There was a wooden box on top of the wardrobe. I'd never touched it before. She said it held "blessings from Zaka."

Inside was a cracked photo of Maïa, younger than I remembered, a dried leaf wrapped in thread and a folded letter—not addressed to me.

The letter read:

"If the fire returns, she'll come with it.

I tried to keep her quiet. I tried to make her forget.

But Maïa was never meant to be silent.

You'll hear her before you see her."

Signed: Your brother.

—Uncle Yannis

***

I sat on the floor.

Cold. Still.

For the first time, I wondered if we hadn't just lost Maïa.

Maybe we'd sacrificed her.

Chapter 17

The station was half-empty when I stormed in.

Ravi looked up from his desk like he'd been waiting for this moment—or dreading it.

"Who else was on the Maïa case?" I asked.

"I told you—"

"Not the files. The *truth*. Who buried her? Who signed off on it? And who signed my uncle's name onto a death report without a body?"

He didn't answer.

"You weren't in charge then. But someone was."

I dropped the locket on his desk again. Not gently this time.

The name hit like an old bruise. Not because it was new. But because he'd carried it too long without speaking it aloud.

"The glyph keeps reappearing. And someone made it sacred. Someone wrote it down *before it ever showed up on those bodies.*"

"Who, Ravi?"

He stared at it for a long time.

Then finally—

"Chief Mervin Soopayah."

"Your mentor."

"He ran everything. The girl. The fire. The files. He handled it all."

I stepped back. Cold fury humming just under my skin.

"Is he still alive?"

"He's retired."

"Then let's talk to him."

"No."

"Why not?"

"Because the last time someone tried, they ended up *disappearing from the island registry three months later. They* weren't erased. They just... stopped being found."

***

I went without Amaya. The house looked the same as it did twenty years ago.

A low bungalow on the hill above Port Royal. Cane fields around it. Crows on the roof. Curtains that never moved.

I knocked once.

The door opened before I could knock again.

"I wondered when you'd come," Mervin said.

He looked smaller now. But not weaker.

The kind of small that condenses everything sharp inside.

* * *

We sat in silence for a while. He poured tea. Didn't drink it.

"She's asking questions," I said finally.

"She was always going to."

"You signed off on her uncle's death."

"I signed what needed to be signed."

"And the glyph?"

"Don't ask about the glyph, Ravi."

"I'm not the one asking."

Mervin finally looked at me.

"Then tell her this:

The island doesn't speak in words.

It speaks in silence.

And some things aren't meant to echo."

***

He slid a file folder across the table.

I opened it.

Inside was a burned map, a school photo

and a name I hadn't seen in years:

Maïa R. Saran — Transferred, not Deceased.

Last known address: Restricted.

Chapter 18

He didn't come back until late.

Ravi walked into the station like the night had dragged him backward through the past. His coat smelled like smoke and old sugarcane. His eyes didn't look at me directly.

"I spoke to him," he said.

"Your mentor?"

"Mervin."

"And?"

"He told me the fire was real."

***

We sat down in the briefing room—just the two of us. The whiteboard still held the glyph.

It had smudged slightly. Like even the marker didn't want to stay clean anymore.

"Your uncle got involved in things he didn't fully understand," Ravi said.

"Maïa too. They believed the old stories. The roots beneath the island. The god that sleeps. That Zaka wasn't just a spirit of work and earth, but... something deeper. Something waiting."

He paused.

"They weren't wrong. But they weren't careful."

***

"What happened to them?" I asked.

"Your uncle died in the fire. That part's true."

"And Maïa?"

"She was supposed to be transferred off-island. For her safety."

"That's not a yes or a no."

He didn't answer right away.

"I don't know what happened to her after that. All I know is... someone went to great lengths to make sure her name disappeared."

***

"Do you believe she's still alive?"

He met my eyes.

"I believe you're not the only one looking for her."

And for the first time in years, he hated how heavy the badge felt.

***

He left me with that.

No folder. No name.

Just enough flame to keep me burning.

***

What Ravi didn't tell me:

That he had a file in his coat pocket.

That it listed Maïa's transfer date, last known location, and a scanned ID photo with a fake name.

And that the note paper-clipped to it read:

"If you hand this to her, the fire spreads."

Chapter 19

The forensics lab behind the Port Lumière station was more shed than science centre. Half the equipment rattled, the fridge hummed louder than the lights, and the microscope had one good eye.

But Ti-Sav made it work.

She moved through the chaos like a storm that knew exactly which papers to blow off the table.

***

I stood over Luc Garnier's personal effects, gloves on. Ti-Sav leaned over the sample tray, squinting at the residue scraped from his shirt collar.

"Does this look like soot to you?" she asked.

"Could be from the boat," I said. "He was found at the docks."

She shook her head. "Boat soot doesn't sparkle."

She held the slide to the light.

"See that shimmer? That's longanis root. Burned, crushed, mixed with oil—same stuff old healers used for 'nocturnal protection.'"

"Protection against what?"

"Whatever doesn't knock."

***

I turned to the parchment pulled from his hand—partially burned, ink flaked at the corners.

"Cinnamon oil, charcoal, iron oxide," I muttered.

Ti-Sav nodded. "Ritual ink."

"Same mix as Laroque's."

"Which means..."

"Whoever killed them is escalating."

***

She moved to the fibre scope and started typing without looking up.

"You know, when you first came back, I figured you were here to prove you were better than us."

"And now?"

"Now I think you're here because you're afraid of what you left behind."

I said nothing.

She kept typing.

"You left. She didn't."

"She?"

"Maïa."

***

That was Ti-Sav.

She didn't say much.

But she always knew when to drop the match.

***

She slid a folder across the table. Garnier's last phone calls. A number he dialled six times in one hour the night before he died.

"I traced it to a burner phone," she said. "Registered under a fake name."

"What name?"

"Yannis."

I stared at her.

"That's not the weird part," she added.

"What is?"

"It pinged from the Saint-Amour Forest. Four days ago."

Chapter 20

Ti-Sav didn't say anything at first.

She just let the data load. She let the glow of the screen flicker between us, like a candle in a wind neither of us wanted to admit was real.

"You're quiet," I said.

"You're not."

"That's new."

"So is watching you fall apart over evidence that hasn't even bled yet."

***

I turned away. But she was already in motion—folding her arms, leaning on the edge of the desk.

"You knew her well."

"It was a long time ago."

"So were most ghosts."

∗∗∗

I didn't answer. I checked the call logs again. Typed. Rewound.

"Look, I get it," she said, softer now.

"Some people you never forget. Especially when they vanish. Especially when the adults in your life *let them vanish.*"

She let that hang.

I looked at her. Finally.

"She's not just a memory."

"I know."

∗∗∗

A beat passed.

"Do you think she's still alive?" Ti-Sav asked.

I almost said no.

But my silence said yes.

"If she is," I whispered,

"Then this isn't just about solving a case.

It's about finding the girl who was punished for remembering something everyone else wanted to forget."

* * *

The door creaked across the room.

Ravi.

He stood there for a second too long, watching us.

Not listening. Just calculating.

He didn't ask what we were looking at.

He already knew.

Chapter 21

Luc Garnier's tablet had been in evidence lockdown since his death.

It took Ti-Sav two hours, a cracked-forensics tool, and a USB cable she called "the stubborn snake" to crack it.

What we found wasn't vacation photos.

It was an encrypted folder marked simply:

Z-Essence Dev. // Off-Island

***

She decrypted it.

Up came topographic overlays, old zoning documents and development projections labelled "Cultural Integration Opportunities"

But the gold was in the land registry scan.

"He wasn't just buying land," Ti-Sav muttered.

"He was targeting sacred zones."

***

She pulled up Yannis's original journal map and overlaid it.

"Look."

"What?"

"Here."

She circled a region marked in red on both maps—once called Bois-Cendre.

"That's the Zone Rouge. Off-limits since the 1987 fire."

"The one near Saint-Amour?"

"Yep. Same place your uncle marked as Ritual Site 3."

***

I leaned in.

"Garnier and Laroque were trying to develop a luxury retreat there."

"Without permits," Ti-Sav said. "Without respect."

She clicked to the next file.

A draft email—unsent.

It read:

"Z.L. has confirmed our window. He says the healer will stay silent. Begin land clearance as scheduled."

Ti-Sav leaned closer, reading aloud. Her voice dropped on the initials.

"Z.L...."

She glanced at me. "That's not Laroque, is it?"

I shook my head slowly.

Ravi hadn't said a word since the initials appeared. But his shoulders were tight. Like the past had reached out and grabbed his spine.

"No. Garnier was writing *to* Laroque."

"So Z.L. is someone else."

"Someone above them both."

She frowned. "You think Z.L. is the one running this?"

"No," I said.

"Z.L. is the one holding the lock."

***

We stared at the screen.

The map.

The shrine.

The initials.

None of them should have touched.

But they did.

***

And whoever Z.L. was—they had power.

The kind that could buy silence.

The kind that could erase land laws.

The kind that could make a girl disappear.

And they were still alive.

Chapter 22

We stared at the draft email for another minute.

The initials glowed like a curse under forensic light.

Z.L.

"Z... who?" Ti-Sav muttered. "Zacharie? Zoë? Zamir?"

"Zane Laroque?" I guessed.

"Cousin?"

"Dead. Years ago."

We ran through more names.

Zaline.

Zubair.

Zhao.

Zubeda.

Nothing stuck. Nothing *felt* right.

					***

"Too careful," I said.

"If someone wanted to hide their name, they'd use initials. But these? They're too clean. Too institutional."

Ti-Sav looked up.

"Like a business."

I froze.

"Z.L. isn't a person," I said slowly.

"It's a corporation."

					***

We jumped on the old station desktop.

Ti-Sav tapped in a search to the Isle de Zaka Corporate Registry—a battered government site that hadn't been updated since dial-up days.

"Here," she said, after three minutes of loading and one crash.

"Zaka Legacy Holdings. Incorporated eighteen years ago. Office registered in Port Royal. No contact number. No active website."

"That's our Z.L."

***

The listed director?

C. Desforges.

I blinked.

"Desforges. That's a name from..."

"The old land arbitration board," Ti-Sav finished.

"They ruled on sacred site usage after the '87 fire."

***

We looked at each other.

"You think he's still around?"

"If he's not," she said,

"someone's still signing for the company."

Behind us, Ravi didn't move.

He just exhaled—long and low—like the name Desforges still burned through him.

Chapter 23

The morning air was heavier than it should've been.

The sky over Port Lumière threatened rain, but didn't deliver. Somewhere behind us, a rooster crowed late. A dog barked in the distance, unanswered. Even the wind felt like it was waiting for something.

So were we.

***

I stood outside the old archives building with Ti-Sav and Ravi.

Inside, a dusty records clerk named Maude was pulling land registration files on Zaka Legacy Holdings.

Ti-Sav bounced on her heels like she'd had too much sugar. Or fury.

"You think they're real?" she asked.

"The company?" I replied. "Oh, they're real. They're just hiding in plain sight."

✳✳✳

Maude returned, breathless and triumphant, holding a slim black file.

"Only what's public," she warned. "But that name—Desforges? He's not listed anymore."

"When did he disappear from the board?" Ravi asked.

"Eighteen months ago," she said. "Replaced by someone using a pseudonym: M. S. Ashvin."

✳✳✳

I turned sharply. "Ashvin?"

Ravi's face didn't change. But his silence deepened.

"What?" I asked him.

"Ashvin was Desforges' second-in-command. Land claims specialist. Vanished after a corruption probe seven years ago."

"And no one brought him back for questioning?"

"No one wanted to," Ravi said. "He had friends in every ministry."

***

We left the archives with more questions than answers—but with something real in our hands.

A footprint.

A pattern.

A thread that didn't want to be pulled.

***

Back in the car, I glanced at Ravi.

He hadn't spoken much. His jaw was set, but his shoulders had dropped. He looked older in the daylight. Not tired—*weathered.*

"You're quiet," I said.

"So are a lot of people," he replied.

"But you're not a lot of people."

***

He turned to me at the next red light.

"There's a reason they let me stay, Amaya," he said. "It wasn't loyalty. It was leverage. They think I'll protect the past because I'm part of it."

"Are you?" I asked.

"I used to be."

A pause.

"But I've been watching you burn through the silence. And I realized... maybe that's what I should've done from the beginning."

***

We didn't speak for the next few blocks.

"You still wearing the badge," I said.

"Yeah," he nodded.

"But I'm not walking under its shadow anymore."

Chapter 24

I'd read the same page in the journal three times.

Yannis' handwriting was sharp, urgent, the kind of script written by someone afraid they were running out of time—or truth.

"She said the island hears things we try to forget.

I think it remembers her."

***

I traced the ink with one finger.

Maïa's name wasn't on the page. But it didn't have to be.

She was everywhere in Yannis' words.

✳✳✳

We had been seventeen.

She wore jasmine oil on her wrists and tied her hair back with a ribbon made from the lining of her school uniform.

She laughed too loudly.

Cried without shame.

And told me once, under the banyan tree near Saint-Amour,

"The island doesn't forget us, even if we leave.

It just hides the parts it doesn't want the others to see."

✳✳✳

Then one day, she was gone.

The fire came weeks later.

Yannis stopped talking.

The adults muttered things about illness, about cremation. No body.

No goodbye.

Just silence wrapped in ritual.

***

I never believed she died. Not completely.

Not when I saw the photo of her, slipped between Yannis' field notes and pressed leaves.

Not when I saw the glyph again—etched into that wall in Site 2—Maïa's sketchbook glyph, the one she used to draw in the margins of her history notebook.

Not when the scent of jasmine haunted the forest like memory refusing to rot.

* * *

I brought the journal to Ti-Sav that afternoon.

She sat in her corner of the lab, eyes scanning logs, hair tied up in frustration.

"This is about Maïa, isn't it?" she said without looking up.

"It's always been about Maïa," I replied.

She flipped through the pages slowly, fingers brushing the aging paper like it could burn her.

"So, what do we do?"

"We follow the glyph."

"And if we find her?"

"Then we ask what else the island buried."

Chapter 25

We laid out the maps like offerings.

Ti-Sav had borrowed municipal records from her cousin at the surveyor's office — nothing digital, just old, crinkled plot overlays and land transfer documents that smelled like mildew and dried sweat.

"Start with what we know," she said, tapping her pen against the edge of her clipboard.

I circled the sites:

- Zaka Essence, where Jean-Michel Laroque was found with his lungs cooked and eyes burned clean
- The coastal grove, still blackened around the roots of the prayer tree

- The forest cave — Site 2 — where Yannis once took me, and where the scent of jasmine hadn't left

- And the narrow bluff overlooking Saint-Amour, where a second glyph had been spotted but nobody had followed. Yet.

"These are the places where the glyph appeared," I said. "Every one of them."

Ti-Sav nodded. She pulled a transparent overlay from the folder and smoothed it across the map.

Parcel boundaries. Purchase dates. Permits in blue ink.

"Now look," she said.

I leaned closer.

Each marked glyph site had a new code scrawled nearby — land titles that hadn't existed ten years ago. New owners. Corporate shells. All bearing some variation of Z.L., or names known to connect back to Zaka Legacy Holdings.

"Z.L. didn't just buy these places," I said.

"They bought places that were already marked."

Ti-Sav squinted at the permit dates.

"Some of these—like the cave site—that land's been untouched for decades."

"Exactly," I said. "And the glyph was already there."

She paused, then pointed to Zaka Essence and the grove.

"But here... they bought the land, then the glyphs appeared. After the permits."

"So, it's not linear," I said. "It's layered.

Some were already sacred. Some were *made sacred again.*"

She looked back at the map. Quiet.

"Or maybe... they're marking the places that should never have been bought in the first place."

***

Outside, a rooster screamed. The sun had begun to drop, slanting red across the edge of the forest line.

We were chasing a killer.

But the island wasn't just bleeding bodies.

It was coughing up its past.

Chapter 26

The light from the desk lamp was flickering again — island voltage, always nervous.

I'd read the journal three times before. But not like this.

This time, I was looking for what wasn't there.

***

Between Yannis' field sketches and folklore citations, a folded page had come loose. Tucked into the binding like a secret too shy to speak.

A hand-drawn map. Not professional. Not clean.

But precise.

Three red circles. One for the grove. One for the cave. One I didn't recognize.

Northern basin.

I stared at the name again:

Bol Gran Zom.

The Big Man's Bowl.

It wasn't on any tourist map. No resorts nearby. Just an old water basin with bad stories wrapped around it like vines.

In the journal, Yannis had underlined just one sentence:

"Maïa said they used the space wrong. Not a prayer. Not a ritual. Something broken."

She drew everything.

But not that place.

Not once.

***

Twenty minutes later, I was sitting in the back garden behind the police dorms, the map spread across a faded plastic table, a flashlight held between two mugs of too-sweet coffee.

Ti-Sav leaned over it, damp curls tied up in a loose bun, thumb pressed against the red circle.

"You sure this is where it is?" she whispered.

"Yannis marked it himself. And Maïa..." I tapped the quote. "She told him something happened there."

Ti-Sav frowned. "I've only heard about this place once. My gran said it was a hollow that burned without fire. Some old priest warned her not to walk barefoot near it."

"Because it was sacred?"

"Because it wasn't," she said. "She said it used to be holy. But something twisted it."

We sat in silence, listening to the cicadas rise and fall. Far off, a dog barked once and fell quiet again.

"Have any developers circled the land?"

Ti-Sav pulled out her phone. "Wait."

She scrolled for a moment, frowning, then held it out to me.

"Look. Registered inquiry from three weeks ago. ZakaLand Holdings. But guess who's listed as director?"

She zoomed in.

Luc's name blinked back at me.

She nodded. "They're going after all the sites. One by one."

"Same places Yannis circled and wrote about."

I leaned back in the chair, staring up at the stars. They looked too clean tonight.

Ti-Sav sipped her coffee. "We going there tomorrow?"

I nodded.

She didn't smile.

Just said, "Good. I'll bring salt and gloves."

Chapter 27

We set out before sunrise.

The kind of dawn where the light doesn't rise — it creeps. As if the sun's trying not to wake anything.

Kiki had lent us the jeep. It smelled like sugarcane rum and sandalwood, and the glovebox was filled with broken rosaries and chewed pen caps.

"You believe in omens?" Ti-Sav asked as we bumped over the gravel road.

"I believe in brake failure," I said.

She laughed, then went quiet again. We didn't talk much after that.

The closer we got to the northern basin, the quieter the island felt — like even the birds didn't want to interrupt.

✳✳✳

Bol Gran Zom wasn't marked.

Not on GPS. Not on Zaka's digital registry. Not on any topographical maps from the last twenty years.

But the shape was still there — a shallow crater surrounded by thick banyans, a natural amphitheatre eaten at the edges by forest. The air had weight. Humid. Sweet with decay.

We stepped out slowly.

No signage. No fences. Just old stone blocks half-buried in vine and moss.

"I think this used to be a public water catchment," Ti-Sav said. "Old French engineering. Abandoned after the floods."

"But someone came back."

I pointed at the ground.

The glyph was there — not burned, not painted.

Carved.

Into the stone slab at the centre. Faint, but deep. Weathered but undeniable.

A jagged flame spiralling into a bowl. The same loop Maïa used to draw. The same shape in the journal. Only older.

Much older.

I crouched, brushed moss from the edge.

"It's not new," I said. "This has been here for years."

"Maybe decades."

Ti-Sav crouched beside me. "Yannis didn't say how he found this?"

"No. But he circled it. And Maïa mentioned it once. That's all I've got."

A bird shrieked overhead. Something white darted through the canopy — a ghost heron, or something pretending to be one.

Ti-Sav stood. "There's more," she said. "Back here."

She led me to the edge of the basin where a cluster of rocks formed a low, broken wall. Hidden behind it — half-buried — was what looked like the edge of a suitcase. Old. Metal clasps corroded green.

We knelt.

She pulled gloves from her bag, handed me a pair. "Found object protocol?"

"Always."

Together, we lifted it free.

The lock cracked with one twist.

Inside: bones.

Small.

Animal.

Arranged in a circle.

At the centre — a scrap of red cloth, and something blackened with soot.

Not burnt.

Branded.

The glyph.

Again.

Ti-Sav didn't speak. Neither did I.

Not yet.

The island was telling a story.

And we weren't at the end yet.

Chapter 28

By the time we returned to the station, the sun was high and too hot. Zaka's heat had teeth today — the kind that clung to the back of your neck, whispering things you didn't want to hear.

We didn't speak in the car.

Not because we didn't have things to say.

But because neither of us wanted to be the first to say them.

***

The lab smelled like metal and bleach — comfort, in its own sterile way.

Ti-Sav laid out the contents of the suitcase like a ritual. The bones. The cloth. The scorched glyph.

I washed my hands twice, then leaned in.

"Juvenile goat," I said, pointing at the skull. "Ritual or mimic ritual. But amateur. Not clean."

"Maybe it wasn't meant to be clean."

She passed me the cloth. I held it under the magnifier.

The weave was old. Handmade. Red dye uneven. I ran a quick test — cochineal-based. Local. At least two decades old.

She watched me closely.

"You're thinking it's connected to Maïa."

"I'm thinking it was meant to be found. Eventually."

"Why?"

"Because someone left a story here. One that never made it to the ending."

I reached for the burned piece of cloth with the glyph.

"It's not a warning. It's a *signature*."

***

We sat down. Laid out everything we knew on the board.

Jean-Michel — dead, burned from the inside.

Luc — Z.L. director, dead too.

Maïa — vanished, never confirmed dead.

Yannis — dead, journal full of red circles and warnings.

The glyph — burned, carved, branded — in all the wrong places.

The dots were connecting.

But the lines weren't straight.

***

Ravi stepped into the doorway. Silent for a second too long.

"You went to the basin."

It wasn't a question.

I didn't look up. "We did."

"You weren't supposed to."

"We weren't supposed to find bones either."

That silenced him.

Finally, he stepped forward, looked at the photos.

He didn't touch anything.

But I saw his eyes track the glyph. The suitcase. The circle of bones.

And I saw it — the recognition.

The fear.

Not of what we'd found.

But of what he'd known.

"What else is missing, Ravi?" I asked quietly.

He didn't answer.

But his hands clenched.

Like he wanted to grab something.

Or maybe, let something go.

Chapter 29

He hadn't smoked in seven years.

Not since the last time he buried evidence under his conscience and called it loyalty.

But tonight, Ravi Caderamen stood alone behind the station, wind slicing through his shirt sleeves, a cheap cigarette trembling between his fingers.

He didn't light it.

Just held it like a relic of an older version of himself — the version who still believed duty meant silence.

***

Mervin's voice came back like fog — soft, slow, dangerous.

"You want to last in this job, Ravi? You keep your eyes on the crime and your hands out of the shadows. Let the old ghosts stay buried."

Mervin had taught him how to file reports that omitted just enough. How to nod when developers smiled. How to let sacred ground be "reclassified" for economic progress.

How to look away.

But the glyph wouldn't let him.

That damned flame had come back to scorch everything.

And this time, someone else was watching.

Amaya.

She'd looked at him like she already knew.

Like she wasn't afraid to dig up what he'd buried.

And Ti-Sav... she was starting to look at him the same way.

Not with respect.

With doubt.

***

He slid the cigarette back into the pack.

Couldn't protect a mentor who didn't deserve the word. Couldn't play both sides anymore.

He stepped back inside.

The squad room was empty, humming low with the sound of old guilt.

Ravi opened his locker.

Pulled out the file he'd hidden there five years ago.

Not a murder case.

A complaint.

Filed by Dr. Yannis Zarin.

A report of unauthorised site clearings near Bol Gran Zom. Of markings erased. Offer letters pushed under doors. Shadows digging in sacred land.

Mervin had told him to ignore it. "He's just a folklorist with a chip on his shoulder."

But now, Ravi read it again — and saw the pattern.

The same places.

The same warnings.

Ignored. Bought. Marked.

Burned.

Then he picked up his phone.

Dialled Amaya.

She answered on the second ring. "Ravi?"

He didn't waste time.

"I have something to show you."

A pause. "Where?"

"My place. Twenty minutes."

"Are you ready?"

"No," he said honestly. "But I'm done running."

Chapter 30

Amaya arrived just before midnight.

The police dorms were dead quiet, the sodium lights flickering like tired ghosts. Ravi opened the door before she knocked.

She looked at him—really looked—and something in her jaw relaxed. Or maybe tensed. Hard to tell these days.

"You said you had something," she said.

Ravi nodded. "Inside."

***

He didn't offer tea.

Didn't clear the cluttered desk, or the old incense ash clinging to the edges of the shrine near his bed. Just pulled out a battered file, placed it between them, and opened it.

Amaya's eyes flicked down.

"Yannis?"

Ravi nodded once.

"Five years ago," he said. "He came to the station. Said he'd seen men surveying the northern basin—Bol Gran Zom. Said they weren't just looking. They were marking. Stripping trees. Moving stones with inscriptions."

Amaya's voice was low. "And?"

"I filed it. Not as a criminal report. As a land use complaint. Mervin had final say." He paused. "He shelved it."

"Why?"

Ravi exhaled. "Because ZL had just registered two shell companies. And someone had given verbal assurances that that basin was... flexible."

Amaya sat back, arms crossed. "So, you let it go."

"I was junior," Ravi said. "Green. Still thinking justice wore uniforms and wrote memos."

"You knew something was wrong."

"I did. And I didn't look again until now."

He pushed another paper toward her—a site registry form.

ZakaLand Holdings. Signed by Luc. Dated two months ago.

"It's the same circle from your map. Your uncle was trying to stop it even before we knew what it was."

Amaya's fingers hovered over the signature.

"The glyph was there," she whispered. "Even back then. I just didn't see it."

Ravi looked down.

"Maybe neither did I."

Amaya's eyes didn't soften.

"You had this for five years, Ravi."

Her voice wasn't raised, but it cut.

"You shelved it. Let them erase him while he was still alive."

"I didn't shelve it," Ravi said. "I let it be shelved."

"Same thing."

He didn't deny it.

"You knew my uncle," she whispered. "You knew he wouldn't invent something just to stir trouble."

"I know that now."

"Now," she repeated. "Convenient."

She stood, moved toward the window like she needed air that hadn't passed through that file.

"You don't get to walk back into this like you were on the right side the whole time."

"I'm not trying to," Ravi said. "I'm just trying to stop what's still happening."

***

They sat in silence. Long enough for the fan to start clicking in protest.

Finally, Amaya spoke.

"Why tell me now?"

Ravi met her eyes. "Because I'm done protecting the dead who don't deserve it. And I think your uncle was silenced before he could go public."

A pause.

"You think they killed him?"

"I think he got too close. Maybe not murdered. But pushed. Pressured. Cornered. And whoever's behind ZL… they don't leave witnesses."

Amaya looked down at the file again.

"There's still one site left," she said softly. "Bol Gran Zom."

He nodded.

"And that's where we go next."

Chapter 31

The crater was quieter the second time.

No ropes, no officers. Just wind moving through tall grass and the weight of something left too long in silence. Ravi had insisted we come back before light faded—said there was more we hadn't seen.

But now, standing at the edge again, it felt like the place had already told us everything.

Or maybe it was just waiting.

Ti-Sav crouched near the rim, brushing at the earth where they'd found the remains. Her gloves were dirt-smudged. Focused. Like she was still listening for the bones.

Ravi stood behind her, arms folded, looking down into the basin. Not like a cop. Like a man trying to remember what he forgot.

"I never came here back then," he said quietly. "I read the file Yannis submitted. Skimmed it. Thought it was folklore. Sites like these... they get dismissed."

"But the glyph was here," I said. "Even back then."

He nodded, jaw tight. "I didn't know what it meant. We told Yannis not to follow up without clearance. Then the application to buy this land went through. I was told it wasn't our concern."

"And you didn't push."

"I was junior. Mervin said let it go."

We were quiet for a while. The basin below shimmered with heat. One edge looked newer—earth darker, a shallow dent where grass hadn't regrown.

Ti-Sav moved to it, knelt.

"Something was buried here recently," she said. "Not bones. Something small. Maybe taken after."

Ravi joined her. "Could've been an offering. Or a message."

Amaya crouched near the roots of the old banyan again. "There's something caught here," she muttered.

Ti-Sav knelt beside her, helping pull away debris. A piece of decayed cloth, tough like burlap but singed at the edge, came free.

Dark stains marred its corner—dried, almost indistinguishable from earth. But not to her eye.

"This is blood," Amaya said quietly.

"Old," Ti-Sav added, "but not gone."

Amaya bagged it carefully. "If we're lucky, it held on to a truth."

"I'm not sure this is over," I said. "Whatever ZL's doing... it's not just land grabs. They're following something. And it started here."

Ti-Sav stood up. "But why start here?"

I hesitated.

"There's something in Yannis' journal," I said. "A line about Maïa. He wrote she'd gone near the basin. That she didn't want to talk about it. Said she'd already told someone."

Ti-Sav looked at me. "Who?"

"I don't know. But if it wasn't her parents... and she didn't want to tell Yannis..."

Ravi tilted his head. "Then who?"

I took a breath.

"She had an art teacher," I said. "Madame Linoré. She always encouraged Maïa's drawing. Never judged it. Maïa said once that drawing was how she made sense of what she couldn't say."

"You think she confided in her?" Ti-Sav asked.

"If she told anyone... it would've been her."

We looked at each other.

Then Ti-Sav broke the silence: "So what are we waiting for?"

Chapter 32

The house looked like it had once been coral-pink.

Now it was mostly vines and rusted iron, the gate leaning like it had given up long ago. A faded bell hung crooked beside the door, the clapper long stolen by the wind or a bored child.

Ti-Sav rang anyway.

Footsteps shuffled inside. Slow. Deliberate. Then the door opened just enough for one wary eye to peer through the gap.

"Oui?"

"Madame Linoré?" I asked, stepping forward. "My name is Amaya Zarin. I... I was a friend of Maïa."

The door opened a little wider.

She looked older than I remembered—silver hair pulled into a loose braid, skin papery with time, but her eyes were still the same. Sharp. Kind. Alert.

"You look like her," she said softly. "Different fire. Same storm."

She stepped aside. "Come in."

***

The inside of her house was cluttered but careful. Books piled in corners. Dried flowers in jars. Paintings leaned against walls, half-finished, full of red and water and things unnamed.

She poured tea without asking and sat with us on a low couch that creaked with the weight of memory.

"You said Maïa," she said, eyes on me. "Why now?"

"She's part of something we're investigating," I said. "I think she saw something. Maybe here. Near Bol Gran Zom."

Madame Linoré flinched. Just slightly. But she did.

"She was scared," she said at last.

"She used to draw lotuses," Madame Linoré said, tapping the edge of a yellowed sketch. "Hundreds of them. It was how she calmed her mind."

The teacher's fingers paused over the paper. "The last few weeks before she disappeared … she stopped. I asked her why."

She hesitated.

"Maïa said something changed. That lotuses belonged to light. And she was seeing too much shadow."

"She was scared more than I'd ever seen her. Came in with charcoal on her fingers and tears she refused to explain. Drew in silence for an hour. Then handed me a page."

"Do you still have it?" Ti-Sav asked gently.

"No," she said. "She took it back the next day. Said it was a mistake."

"What did it show?" I asked.

She hesitated. "It wasn't the basin. Not really. It was... people in a circle. But no faces. Just hollow eyes and fire underneath. And one shape above it all. A spiral. Like the one you find in storm shells. Or the one you see in the sand when something has burrowed deep and left no trace."

My breath hitched. "The glyph?"

She didn't speak for a moment. Then: "Yes. But not quite. Not fully formed. As if she'd seen it but couldn't draw it whole."

"Did she say anything?" Ti-Sav asked.

Madame Linoré looked down into her teacup. "Only that someone had told her to forget. That if she didn't, she'd disappear like the others."

"Others?"

She shook her head. "I thought it was adolescent melodrama. But now..." Her voice trembled. "I should've listened harder."

We sat in silence.

Ravi, who had been quiet the whole time, finally spoke. "Did she mention who told her that?"

"No names," she said. "But she was frightened. She said it wasn't the dead that haunted her. It was the living."

***

We left with a photo from their final school year—Maïa at seventeen, hair wilder than I remembered, her smile half-finished. She stood just behind me. I didn't know it then, but it was the last photo ever taken of her alive.

And as we walked back toward the car, Ti-Sav murmured, "If this thing started twenty years ago, maybe Maïa wasn't the first ghost after all."

Chapter 33

The photo sat on my desk beside Yannis' journal, their edges misaligned like puzzle pieces from different boxes.

Maïa's face. Seventeen. Same wild hair, but the light in her eyes had changed. It wasn't just age.

It was fear.

Ti-Sav had gone to file the official visit notes. Ravi had disappeared again, not saying where. Maybe chasing his conscience. Or running from it.

I stared at the old school photo. My hand hovered over Maïa's image, as if touching her could rewind time.

Yannis had written so little about her final visits.

One cryptic line:

"She stopped drawing fire. Said it was too close now. Said it remembered."

I pulled the journal toward me. There was something in the way he phrased that—like he didn't believe it, but didn't dismiss it either.

Then I saw the margin.

A faint smudge. Ink, but different from his usual black. I tilted the page into the desk light.

It wasn't a glyph.

It was a partial name.

Or rather, an initial and a scrawl:

L. Des —

The rest was cut off by the edge of the paper.

L. Des…

Luc Desjardins?

It wasn't proof. But it was a fracture.

I pulled up Ti-Sav's notes from the Bol Gran Zom basin.

Luc's name was listed as director on the ZakaLand inquiry.

Maïa's fear. Yannis' warnings. Luc's signature.

And the basin marked again.

I opened a fresh page in my notebook.

Drew the glyph in red ink. Wrote the names:

- Jean-Michel Laroque
- Luc Desjardins
- Maïa
- Yannis
- ZakaLand Holdings

I circled the ones still breathing.

Then I circled *Ravi*.

Because silence is its own kind of signature.

Chapter 34

The email came just after midnight.

No subject line. No letterhead. Just a crisp, formal paragraph dressed in false civility:

"Dr. Zarin, we appreciate your contribution to the ongoing investigation. That said, certain leads — particularly those tied to historical folklore or land ownership — risk diverting focus from the official scope of inquiry. We trust the Zakan authorities will continue to lead the matter professionally. We advise caution before linking unrelated matters in ways that could affect public confidence or impede future land development."

A warning pretending to be a thank-you note.

I read it twice. Forwarded it to no one.

Instead, I walked down to the field tent behind the precinct, where the portable generator hummed like a nervous heart. Ti-Sav was bent over the site logs, the light from her headlamp bouncing off her glasses.

She glanced up as I approached, read my face, and muttered, "What now?"

I passed her my phone. She scanned the screen, her brow darkening with every line.

"Seriously? They're pulling the 'hysterical consultant' card now?" she hissed. "Classic move. Warm up to you in public, slap your wrists in private."

"They're trying to make this about me," I said. "Not the bodies. Not the glyphs. Not the company whose name keeps showing up."

Ti-Sav set the phone down like it was something she wanted to smash. "They think you're on a witch hunt."

"They should be more worried about the witches finding *them*."

We sat in silence for a moment, the buzz of moths tapping against the plastic lantern filling the space. Then Ti-Sav poured me a cup of instant coffee, her hands still steady despite the anger flickering behind her eyes.

"Do we slow down?" she asked.

"No," I said. "We go quieter."

Later that morning, Ravi asked to speak with me.

We were at the precinct's back lot, the sun already high, humidity clinging like guilt. He didn't bring tea. He didn't smile.

"You got a message," he said.

"You read my inbox now?"

"No. But I know when the Ministry gets nervous. And I know when they send… reminders."

I met his gaze. "They told me to stay in my lane."

He exhaled through his nose. "They're scared."

"Of what?"

He didn't answer. Just looked past me at the distant rise of the northern hills. "This isn't about one hotel developer. Or one missing girl. It's about what happens when people start pulling threads they weren't meant to see."

"Why are you still here, Ravi?" I asked. "Are you protecting something? Or are you watching to see if I make the same mistake you did?"

His jaw tightened. He didn't deny it.

Before he could speak, Ti-Sav appeared at the tent's edge, holding a rolled document.

"You both need to see this."

She unrolled it on the table — an old site registry report, dated two years ago, from an abandoned shrine zone near the western ridge. The title block had been amended twice. But beneath layers of whiteout and annotation, we saw it.

A sketch.

Not quite the glyph. But close.

Angular. Symmetrical. Familiar.

"Where did this come from?" Ravi asked.

"Misfiled under an old forest erosion survey," she said. "I found it while tracing land conversion plans."

"It's not the same," I said. "But it's echoing something."

"Maybe," Ti-Sav said, frowning. "Or maybe it's someone trying to mislead us. Misdirect. Buy time."

I traced the lines with my fingertip, then looked up.

"Doesn't matter. The glyphs, the heat, the silence — it's all leading somewhere. And they want us looking the other way."

Ravi said nothing. But his eyes didn't flinch.

Which meant, for now — he was still on our side.

Chapter 35

The archives in Port Lumière didn't smell like knowledge.

They smelled like mildew and resignation — like paper that had waited too long to be read.

The government building loomed like a repurposed ruin, colonial arches barely holding up under the weight of bureaucracy. We passed through three sets of security without anyone asking the right questions.

Inside, the archivist gave us a smile like a rubber stamp — polite, dry, forgettable.

"You're looking for what kind of files, exactly?"

"Land transfers, zoning reclassifications, restricted site access," Ti-Sav rattled off, already flashing the case authorization like it meant more than it did. "Specifically tied to ZakaLand Holdings. Or anything flagged 'Z.L.'"

The archivist nodded slowly. "You're not the first."

That made us pause.

"Who else?" I asked.

She shook her head. "Didn't give a name. Just handed in a list. Two weeks ago. Quiet man. Local accent. Walked with a cane."

My stomach pinched. "What did he want?"

"Same thing. Sacred sites turned commercial. Especially the ones with contested histories."

Ti-Sav and I exchanged a glance.

Ravi wasn't with us. He was back at the precinct, keeping up the illusion of protocol. Or maybe keeping someone off our backs.

We were on our own.

***

The records weren't digitized. Zaka's paper trail was stubborn — full of handwritten notations, old wax stamps, and photocopies so faded they looked like ghosts.

After two hours of thumbing through parchment, we hit something.

Not a site plan. Not a survey.

A letter.

Typed. Single page. Stamped confidential. Dated eighteen years ago.

To: Regional Inspector of Cultural Preservation

From: Senior Advisor, Heritage and Zoning Board

Re: Unauthorized Ritual Structures and Symbolic Vandalism – North Basin Sector

"Please note continued concerns around the reappearance of markings associated with disputed religious practices at Site 7C — colloquially known as 'Bol Gran Zom.'

As discussed, the prior decision to classify the basin area as ecologically hazardous rather than spiritually protected allows for future zoning reclassification if deemed commercially viable. However, these symbols must be removed promptly.

Do not escalate.

Z.L."

Ti-Sav's voice was low. "They were scrubbing the glyphs off *before* the land got converted."

I touched the letter's edge.

Someone had burned the bottom corner — just enough to blacken the initials. But not enough to erase them.

"Shadow paper," I said.

"What?"

"Documents that were never meant to exist. The kind that live in between categories. Not zoning. Not religion. Not even crime. Just control."

***

As we left the building, the wind off the coast tasted like rust.

Ti-Sav was quiet beside me, her fingers tapping against her thigh — restless, focused.

"They've been preparing this for years," she finally said.

I nodded. "And every time the island tried to whisper the truth — they buried it. Burned it. Bought it."

She glanced sideways. "So, what now?"

I looked ahead — to the road winding inland, to the hills that once held prayers and now held secrets.

"Now," I said, "we listen louder."

Chapter 36

Ravi handed me a slim file.

"This showed up in the early hours," he said. "Found outside your guesthouse. Quietly flagged by one of the juniors. No chain of custody, no official tag."

Inside: a field note. Clinical. No signature.

Unmarked effigy left at doorstep. Cloth wrapping, char pattern consistent with ritual burning. Ash residue includes clove oil, ground Ashoka bark, and coconut fibre. Symbolic elements intact. No visible prints.

Possible warning — or mimic of protection rite reversed.

Request full analysis.

Stapled beside it was the photo: a scorched doll, hollow eyes, red string coiled around the middle like a curse too tight to cut.

The image was grainy. A straw effigy strung up in a flame-scorched grove.

But at the bottom corner—barely visible—was a paper scrap tied to its wrist.

Zoomed in, the letters blurred, but the shape of a line was there.

Writing, maybe. Or just the idea of writing.

A message meant to be seen, not read.

She set the photo down slowly.

"Someone wanted us to find this."

Ti-Sav leaned over. "You've been marked."

"Message is clear," I said. "Back off."

Ravi's voice was low. "They don't want this to go official. Not yet. That's why it came to me directly, without a name."

Ti-Kiki, leaning in the doorway, cocked an eyebrow. "So, you got a creepy gift now too?"

I looked at him. "Too?"

He shrugged. "This island has long arms. And a longer memory. Ask Ravi."

Ravi didn't flinch. "My mentor got one. Years ago. Same type of ash, same threading. Two days later, he was quietly reassigned."

***

Back inside the precinct, the tension was thick enough to drink.

Officer Roopramanien — Ti-Kiki — lounged against the desk like gravity didn't apply to him, sipping on a mystery thermos and watching us like a slow burn.

"Did you see the note in the photo?" Ravi asked quietly.

Amaya nodded. "Barely. Couldn't make the words. But someone wanted us to know it was there."

Ti-Kiki scratched his chin. "Creepy little whisper from the woods. I don't like it."

"Effigy," Ti-Sav said. "Used in some protective rites. But flipped like this — it's a threat."

"Flipped by who?" he asked. "Witch-doctor? Politician? Banker with a hobby?"

"Whoever it was," I said, "they're getting desperate."

Ravi walked over to the evidence board. Pinned the doll photo beneath the glyph.

For a long moment, we stood in silence.

Then he said, "There's something I haven't told you."

Kiki's eyebrows climbed.

Ti-Sav looked up sharply. "Now's the time, Inspector."

Ravi's jaw tightened.

"Luc. He wasn't just a developer. He was once a junior policy analyst — under Mervin. On the cultural advisory board. That's how he learned where the sacred sites were. What was vulnerable."

Ti-Sav muttered something in Creole under her breath.

"And Z.L.?" I asked.

Ravi exhaled. "It started as a shell company. But it wasn't Luc's idea. He just carried it forward."

"Who started it?"

His silence was the answer.

"Let me guess," I said. "Your mentor?"

He nodded once.

"I protected him," he said. "Too long. I thought I owed him. But maybe I just didn't want to admit what I'd become."

***

The precinct lights flickered.

Down the hall, a junior officer's phone rang and stopped. The silence returned like it never left.

We were all marked now.

By guilt. By fire. By the glyphs we had ignored for too long.

Ti-Sav glanced at me. "Still want to keep going?"

I picked up the doll. Held its melted gaze.

"If they're trying to scare us," I said, "they should've tried harder."

Chapter 37

The rain had stopped, but the smell of it lingered—wet bark, clay, and something older. The kind of scent that seeps into skin if you stand still too long.

Ti-Sav sat on the back steps of the station, a cigarette burning low between her fingers. She didn't smoke often, only when something twisted in her gut wouldn't settle.

I joined her, settling beside her on the damp concrete. She didn't look at me right away.

"I don't like effigies," she said after a minute.

"Symbolic or anatomical?"

"Both." A pause. "But mostly the ones that show up on a cop's desk."

I watched the smoke curl from the tip of her cigarette, white tendrils snaking into the night.

"You think it's from the same hand as the glyphs?" I asked.

Ti-Sav shrugged, then flicked the cigarette toward a puddle where it hissed and died. "Maybe not the same hand," she said. "But maybe the same head. Or heart. Some folks carry spirits like debt."

I tilted my head. "You're not talking about Zaka folklore."

She gave a hollow laugh. "Aren't I? My gran used to say some things on this island remember who we used to be. And they don't like who we became."

I didn't answer. I wasn't sure I could.

Inside, the station was too quiet. Ravi stood by the evidence table, staring at the effigy again. He hadn't said much since the note arrived.

"This isn't just about you," he finally said, voice low. "It's about me. This... whatever's coming... I was part of it once. And now it's circling back."

I stepped closer. "Then help me stop it."

He met my eyes, tired but resolute. "I'm trying, Aya. But there are things you don't know. Things I can't say unless I'm ready to burn the whole thing down."

"Then maybe it's time to light the match."

Before he could answer, the lab door clicked open.

"Results are in," said a tech with latex gloves and bloodshot eyes. "From the Bol Gran Zom sample."

We leaned in.

"Cloth fragment. Aged—probably twenty years old or more. Found deep in the root structure. Stained."

My voice came out flat. "Blood?"

The tech nodded. "Very likely. The cloth was preserved enough to hold trace DNA."

Ti-Sav stood beside me, arms folded tight. "Human?"

"Yes. Female markers. The mitochondrial DNA matches the general maternal lineage we've associated with Maïa Saramine's family — same haplogroup, no red flags. But it's not unique. To confirm it's *her*, we'll need a direct maternal sample — like from her mother or a full sibling."

My chest tightened. "Hair? Tissue?"

"A strand of hair was embedded in the cloth weave," the tech said. "We've isolated it, but the profile's degraded. Still, initial markers place it in proximity to Maïa's known maternal genetics."

I stared at the cloth through the glass—burnt at the edges, stubborn in the centre.

Ti-Sav crossed her arms, eyes fixed on the evidence. "So, she was there."

I didn't answer. The cloth said presence.

But it didn't say why.

Chapter 38

The effigy hadn't moved.

But the silence around it felt heavier. Like the island had inhaled and was holding its breath.

Ravi stood with arms folded, eyes fixed on the doll like it might blink.

"I've seen gang threats," he muttered. "Corruption, blackmail. Even voodoo-style warnings on the mainland. But this..." He shook his head. "This feels like a dare."

Ti-Sav crouched, careful not to disturb the dried petals or the salt circle. "So, we agree this wasn't just for show?"

"No," Amaya said. "It's a line in the sand."

She turned the small shell bead between her gloved fingers. "Whoever left it wanted us to know we're getting close. But they're also watching. They know our route. Our pace."

Kiki let out a low whistle. "Or they just know this island better than we do."

"Doubt it," Ravi said, his voice clipped.

They turned, startled at the certainty in his tone.

Amaya met his eyes. "Something you want to share?"

Ravi hesitated. Then nodded slowly.

"I've been talking to Mervin."

Kiki snorted. "That old snake?"

Ravi ignored him. "He confirmed something I suspected. Z.L.'s expansion wasn't random. They're acquiring land that has something underneath. Not gold. Not oil. But... silence. Secrets. The kind you only keep if they're worth something."

"And now someone's trying to bury those secrets again," Amaya said.

Ravi nodded. "Or bury us with them."

Ti-Sav straightened. "Then we need to go back to Bol Gran Zom."

"No," Ravi said, surprising them. "Not yet."

He pulled out a creased folder, the edges smudged with age. Dropped it on the table.

"First, we visit the archive. My mentor's files. The old restricted ones. Mervin gave me access. Or thought he did."

Amaya raised a brow. "What does that mean?"

Ravi's mouth tightened. "He gave me *most* of it. But there's one folder missing."

"Let me guess," Kiki said. "The one labelled 'Maïa'?"

"Not just her. The glyph. And one more name: Yannis Zarin."

Silence fell again.

This time, no one breathed.

Chapter 39

The early light fell through the canopy like stained glass. Bol Gran Zom looked different at dawn—less like a scar in the land, more like a wound that hadn't healed right. Mist curled low, skimming the crater floor as if trying to remember what was buried beneath.

Ti-Sav crouched near the roots. Her gloved hands brushed the soil with surgical precision. "It's fresher here. This patch was disturbed—maybe three, four days ago?"

Ravi stood a few feet back, watching the circle of trees with narrowed eyes. He hadn't spoken much since the photo. Since the effigy. Since the hint that the past wasn't just bleeding—it was pointing.

"I don't get it," Ti-Sav said softly. "If they wanted to scare us, they wouldn't leave a lead."

"Unless the lead is bait," Ravi murmured.

Amaya knelt beside the roots, noting the scorched tips and the slight indentation in the soil. "Or a test. To see if we'll keep digging."

They did.

It took an hour. And then, just beneath the surface, Ti-Sav's trowel struck something hard.

Not bone. Not stone.

Wood.

She brushed away the dirt, revealing the top of a small carved box. Weather-warped but intact, the symbol burned into the lid made all three freeze.

The glyph.

Again.

But smaller. Cleaner. Almost delicate.

Amaya looked at Ravi. "You said it was a warning."

He nodded slowly. "This one feels different."

Ti-Sav cracked open the box.

Inside: a stack of dried leaves, handwritten notes on parchment—weathered but legible—and at the bottom, tucked between the pages—

A photo.

Black and white. Grainy. A girl sitting near a twisted tree.

Maïa.

The same grin. The same jasmine in her hair.

But she wasn't alone.

Two men stood behind her, only half in frame.

One of them, unmistakably, was Luc.

The other... Ravi's breath caught in his throat.

Amaya whispered, "You recognize him?"

Ravi didn't answer.

But the silence said yes.

The glyph wasn't just a warning.

It was a record.

And someone had just reopened the archive.

Chapter 40

The photo stared up from the desk like it had waited twenty years for someone to ask the right question.

Maïa. Two men. One smiling too wide. One not looking at the camera. A banyan tree behind them — the same crooked spine that stood near Bol Gran Zom. The image wasn't sharp, but it was enough.

It was enough to bring bile to the back of my throat.

The photo hadn't been crumpled or creased. It had been cared for. Preserved. Protected. Wrapped in waxed cloth, sealed in a wooden case, hidden where only the roots could remember.

And then buried.

Like a prayer.

Like a sin.

✳✳✳

I held the edges gently — not just for evidence. For reverence. For pain.

"They're older," I said quietly. "Not boys. Men."

Ti-Sav nodded. "Not tourists. Look at their shoes. Their clothes. That's local."

"And Maïa?" My voice almost caught.

She looked young.

But tired.

And her smile... it wasn't her real one. Not the wild grin that always came with mango juice and bad poetry. This one had hesitation stitched into the corners. This was a smile for survival.

Ravi stepped closer, his shadow cutting across the desk like a blade. He didn't touch the photo.

But he looked like he might break anyway.

"She never told anyone," I said. "Not me. Not Yannis. She just... drew."

Ravi's jaw ticked. "Who took the photo?"

"I don't know."

"Who buried it?"

"I don't know that either."

But someone wanted it to be found. Not destroyed. Not lost. Just... delayed. Someone who couldn't carry the truth aboveground, but couldn't bury it forever either.

***

I lifted the photo again. Behind it, burnt carvings inside the box lid.

A faint glyph.

Same shape.

Same pressure.

But older. Maybe the first.

"She didn't draw this," I murmured. "This wasn't Maïa."

Ravi leaned in. "You're sure?"

"Maïa copied it. Traced it. I think... I think she saw it here first."

Ti-Sav exhaled slowly. "So, this isn't just a symbol. It's a signpost. A signature."

"No," I said. "It's a message."

And for the first time, I realized...

Maybe the killer wasn't the only one leaving clues.

Maybe someone was helping us.

Quietly.

From the shadows.

One buried truth at a time.

Chapter 41

The wind off the eastern coast carried salt and smoke. At Zaka Essence, the palm fronds rustled like restless ghosts.

Amaya hadn't intended to come back.

But she stood now at the edge of the property, just past the bamboo grove, where the maintenance path curved like a question mark toward the cliffs. The sea beyond churned, silver and sharp under the morning light.

Ti-Sav joined her, holding a tablet with a flickering screen. "Archives coughed up a name."

Amaya raised an eyebrow.

"Same year as Luc's firm signed the Bol Gran Zom inquiry. A man named Gabriel

Chazan. Junior paralegal. Disappeared. Officially—he resigned. Unofficially—he vanished.”

“Did he work on land deeds?”

Ti-Sav nodded. “Luc signed the papers. Chazan filed them.”

Amaya stared out at the horizon. “And you’re saying this guy disappeared just before the first murder was reported?”

“Three weeks before,” Ti-Sav said quietly.

From behind the resort’s staff wing, a soft sound — almost like a footstep — cracked a branch.

Amaya turned sharply. No one there. But the old talismans strung between the trees were swaying, slow and deliberate. One had snapped again. Just like the first time.

Ti-Sav noticed. “Second one this week.”

They walked on in silence, looping toward the back of the resort.

"I sent the photo to the regional database," Ti-Sav added. "The one with Maïa and the two men."

"And?"

"One of the men is Chazan. The other... still unidentified. Might be a local, might be a ghost."

Amaya stopped.

A faint scratch marked the edge of the wooden fence — fresh, not old weathering. Someone had been here. Recently. Watching, maybe.

Ti-Sav followed her gaze. "We should go. Ravi wants to meet."

"Where?"

"He didn't say."

"Of course he didn't."

Amaya's eyes trailed back to the sea. Somewhere behind that polished infinity pool, someone had burned a man from the inside out. Somewhere in the soil, another person had been left like a secret. And still, something was breathing — not in the lungs of the dead, but in the lies that kept their silence warm.

"We're close," Amaya murmured.

Ti-Sav didn't ask to what.

Chapter 42

The air in the archive room was brittle. Amaya exhaled slowly, the box on the desk before her covered in a light sheen of dust that hadn't settled from today. She reached in, gingerly lifting a folder marked *ZAK-CHAZAN-INQUIRY*. The corner had curled from humidity.

Ravi stood by the open window, his silhouette sharp against the moonlight. Ti-Sav sat cross-legged on the floor, journal open, one hand scribbling notes, the other tugging at her braid.

Amaya flipped open the file. The pages inside were sparse—report summaries, witness statements, two grainy black-and-white photos, and a final report marked:

"Chazan Gabriel. French national. Arrived in Zaka for three months of spiritual retreat and private research. Had a temporary residence permit. Last seen near Rivière Sombre in the northeast. Was documenting 'sacred geographies.'"

"Sacred geographies?" Ti-Sav squinted up. "Sounds like colonialism for 'places we didn't understand but wanted to own.'"

Amaya nodded. "He was looking into geomantic patterns and spiritual energy lines. Folklore meets cartography. He was convinced that certain sites on the island were... active."

Ravi finally spoke, voice low. "He said they pulsed. Called them 'veins of Zaka.'"

Amaya looked up sharply. "You met him?"

He hesitated. "Once. Briefly. Before he disappeared."

A pause.

"You didn't mention this."

"I didn't think it was connected. Then."

Now Ti-Sav looked up, clearly not buying it. But she said nothing.

Amaya returned to the file. Beneath the last page, something caught her attention. A drawing—slipped between the sheets, unsigned, on rice-thin tracing paper.

She held it up to the light.

A basin. Circular. Steep walls. Trees drawn like they leaned away. And at the centre, faint but deliberate—*the glyph.*

Ravi's eyes narrowed. "That wasn't in the file before."

"It is now."

Amaya's voice was even, but her stomach tightened.

"Did Chazan leave this?"

There was no name. No signature. Just a symbol in red pencil on the back: *V2*.

"Version two?" Ti-Sav asked.

"Or Victim two," Amaya murmured.

The room fell silent.

Outside, a dog barked once.

Then nothing.

Chapter 43

The interview room at Zaka Central wasn't much. A fan hummed lazily overhead, its shadow slicing the light across the walls. Amaya crossed her arms. Ti-Sav leaned in the doorway, jaw tight. Ravi sat across from them—not as a superior. As a man ready to be stripped of whatever armour he had left.

"Gabriel Chazan," Amaya said, sliding the name across the table like a challenge. "We found the records. We know he went missing two decades ago."

Ravi didn't flinch. But he didn't look surprised, either.

"I was a junior officer then," he said quietly. "Assigned to assist Mervin in a string of... 'incidents.' Sacred sites. Break-ins. Strange symbols. We were told to treat them as trespassing or local mischief. And Gabriel? He was just a name on a volunteer permit. A researcher. Botanist, supposedly."

Ti-Sav raised a brow. "Supposedly?"

"He was more than that," Ravi said. "He came to Zaka through a private investor linked to ZakaLand Holdings. Even then, the company was circling lands like vultures. Gabriel had access. He was curious—too curious. And then... he vanished."

Amaya's voice was a blade. "And what did you do?"

"I filed the report. Mervin buried it."

He looked at her now, truly looked, and it wasn't a gaze of authority. It was one of reckoning.

"That was the moment I understood this badge doesn't mean what we think it does. I stayed. I rose. I told myself I could do more from inside the system."

"And did you?" Amaya asked.

"I kept you from being shut out, didn't I?" he said, not unkindly. "But no. I didn't stop what came next."

Ti-Sav's voice was softer. "Why now?"

"Because someone's waking up the ghosts. Because this time it's not just old symbols and buried names. It's fire. It's death. And because you two are the only ones who care enough to burn with it if it means getting the truth."

He stood. Pulled a thin, yellowed folder from his coat. "Mervin kept this from the official archive. It's all I could save without being noticed. Chazan's field notes, a copy of a sketch with the glyph... and a list of GPS coordinates. He was tracking the *same sites* Maïa circled in her drawings."

He slid the file across to Amaya. The weight of it felt heavier than it looked.

"I'm with you," Ravi said. "No more secrets. No more games."

Amaya studied him for a long moment.

Then she nodded.

"Welcome to the team," she said. "Now let's find out who lit the match."

Chapter 44

The email was buried in a backup folder labelled *Accounts_Archive_2018*. Not where secrets usually hide—but that's the trick with Luc. He never buried them deep. Just beneath your nose, where you'd never look.

Ti-Sav had stumbled on it while comparing ZakaLand Holdings' acquisition trail with Chazan's glyph timeline.

Now she was holding out her tablet, eyes narrowed. "You need to read this," she told Ravi.

Ravi adjusted his glasses and scrolled.

From: luc.garnier@zakalandholdings.zk

To: m.laurent@equanixconsulting.fr

Subject: Re: Site acquisition approvals

Drafted: 7 May 2018

Status: UNSENT

"We've cleared the cultural review team—they found nothing documented, so we're moving forward.

Site 3 will be acquired quietly. There is one dissenting opinion, but she no longer lives on the island.

If necessary, handle through the mainland partnership.

The glyph is nothing but folklore—no legal bearing.

Let's wrap this before it draws more attention."

Ravi's jaw clenched. "She no longer lives on the island... that's Maïa."

Amaya leaned in, the words like smoke around her. "He never sent it. But he *wrote* it. That's almost worse."

"Why keep a draft?" Ti-Sav muttered. "Was he waiting for the go-ahead... or did someone stop him?"

Ravi ran a hand over his face. "And who the hell is 'the mainland partnership'?"

"Not just one person," Amaya said. "Sounds like an entity. Or a syndicate."

Ti-Kiki, who'd wandered in with two boiled cassava dumplings and zero invitation, added dryly, "Sounds like someone who doesn't want us sniffing further."

Amaya tapped the screen. "Site 3. That's not the grove, the cave, or Bol Gran Zom. That's something else."

"And we don't know what it is *yet*," Ti-Sav said, "but we will. I've got coordinates from Chazan's notebook I haven't placed on the map yet."

Kiki took a bite of dumpling. "If Luc never sent that mail, someone else saw it. Or forced it to stay unsent."

Ravi stared out the window. The light had begun to fade across the bay, shadows climbing the wall like time folding in on itself.

"This isn't just about land anymore," he said.

"No," Amaya whispered. "It's about silencing the past."

Chapter 45

The records room at the Zaka National Archive wasn't as dusty as Ravi remembered. But maybe that was just his guilt clouding the air.

Ti-Sav sneezed twice as they entered, her hands already gloved and notebook out. "Place smells like paper and old secrets."

Amaya didn't speak. She went straight to the request counter, handed over the form Ravi had signed that morning—an expedited search for files related to land acquisition permits, development proposals, and cultural protection exemptions dating back twenty years.

The clerk—a bespectacled man with eyebrows that could take flight—glanced at the names on the form. His lips twitched.

"These are restricted," he said.

"I know," Amaya replied, voice calm.

"They require clearance from—"

"They have it," Ravi cut in. "Signed this morning by the Ministry Liaison's office. Check your fax."

The man gave Ravi a long look. "Fax? What year is this?"

"Zaka," Ti-Sav said. "Time's a spiral."

With a muttered groan, the clerk disappeared into the back room.

***

They waited in silence, the drone of an old ceiling fan the only sound.

Then the clerk returned, pushing a wheeled cart with a single locked file box on it. A yellow tag dangled from the latch.

"CHAZAN: INQUIRY FILE // TEMPORARY HOLD - DO NOT REMOVE"

Amaya's fingers brushed the box as if it might vanish. "We need to copy these. Quickly."

Inside were brittle memos, black-and-white photographs, two taped transcripts of interviews—one with a certain *G. Chazan*, and one labelled "deceased: witness unknown."

Ti-Sav flipped open a file. "He tried to file a claim," she murmured. "Said something illegal happened at the Grove. No one followed up."

"He vanished three weeks later," Ravi added. "Same month Maïa disappeared."

A slow chill threaded up Amaya's spine. "So, they silenced both."

"Or used one to silence the other," Ti-Sav said softly.

At the bottom of the box was a map. Photocopied. With a mark. *A fourth site.*

Not the grove. Not the cave. Not the bowl.

A place they hadn't been yet.

A forgotten estate.

She tapped it with her pen. "Chazan called it *Le Domaine.*"

Ravi leaned over. "It's private land now."

"Whose?" Amaya asked.

He didn't blink.

"ZakaLand Holdings. Transferred title... three months ago."

Chapter 46

The glass of iced ginger tea sweated in Amaya's hand as she flipped through the scanned property records on the veranda of Zaka Essence in the afternoon. Her laptop's screen reflected in the window pane—too bright, too clean for the kind of rot they were circling.

"Maïa Saramine," she said aloud, letting the name taste itself on her tongue. "She was right there, Ti-Sav. In the middle of it. And we were all looking sideways."

Ti-Sav leaned on the railing, a half-empty tea bottle dangling from her fingers. "So, it's hers?"

Amaya, shaking her head, "not quite. It's consistent with the Saramine family's maternal line. Same mitochondrial markers."

"Which means?" asked Ravi.

"Mitochondrial DNA is passed down from mother to child. So, this could be Maïa. But it could also be her mother, an aunt, even a cousin. It doesn't rule her out—but it doesn't confirm her either" said Amaya.

Ti-Sav sighed. "So, we're close."

Amaya confirmed. "We're closer. But we need nuclear DNA to be certain."

Amaya tapped the screen. "The glyph appears near every disputed site. The pattern's too tight to be random. Maïa told Yannis something happened in that basin, but she never drew it. Not once. That's what bothers me."

Ti-Sav sipped her tea. "She could've been scared. Or threatened. Maybe it was the only thing she couldn't draw without pulling the truth out with it."

Amaya's thoughts wandered back to the effigy. To the buried photograph. To the look on Ravi's face when he realized the trap was closing in—not around someone else. Around him.

"Luc Garnier knew too much. ZakaLand Holdings was a shell. But the names it's touched... they're not small. Lawyers. Bureaucrats. Retired ministers. And..."

Ti-Sav raised an eyebrow. "Don't say it."

"... Gabriel Chazan."

Ti-Sav exhaled, slow and sharp. "The first man who disappeared before the first murder. You think they're connected?"

"I think he vanished when Maïa did. And now his ghost is whispering from the digital records no one bothered to wipe properly."

A breeze rustled through the palm leaves. The sound of waves kissing the rocks below.

"You still think she's alive?" Ti-Sav asked.

Amaya didn't answer at first.

She just stared at the screen. At the name.

Saramine.

She whispered, "I think if she is, someone's gone to great lengths to make sure we never find her."

And for the first time, she wasn't sure whether they were hunting a witness.

Or waking something the island buried on purpose.

Chapter 47

The Saramine home sat at the end of a cracked lane lined with frangipani trees, their blossoms falling like memories too soft to hold. The shutters were painted sea-glass green. One hung crooked, like it had forgotten how to close.

No dog barked. No children shouted nearby.

It was the kind of silence that had learned to live with itself.

They walked the last hundred meters in silence, feet crunching the gravel path that led to the old Saramine house.

"They said she slipped at the cascade. That the water took her. But on Zaka, when a body disappears, we don't always believe the cascade is the one doing the taking."

Helicopters came. Search parties. Even dogs.

They found nothing.

Her schoolbag sat on the rock like a ghost had placed it there. Neatly zipped. Dry.

They held a ceremony anyway.

Lit candles. Sang prayers. Laid her favourite dress near the brèdes songes (elephant's ears) lining the cascade.

The official word was: *missing, presumed drowned.*

But no one really believed it. Not then. Not now.

Ti-Sav glanced at me as we stood at the gate. "You sure?"

Ti-Sav exhaled, low. "You ready?"

Amaya nodded.

"No," I said. "But we're here."

I raised a hand to knock. Before I could, the door opened.

A woman stood there. Mid-sixties, maybe. Her hair pulled tight in a silver braid, skin the colour of old teakwood, eyes unreadable. She didn't greet us. Didn't ask our names. Just said,

"You're here about my daughter."

Not a question.

I nodded.

She stepped aside without another word.

Inside, the house was cool and dim, the smell of bay leaf and mothballs hanging in the air. There were no photos on the walls. No signs of time passing. Just one thing above the mantel—an old school drawing, curling at the edges. A banyan tree with roots that reached down into shadows, its branches full of open eyes.

"My name is Shanta Saramine," she said, seating herself in a wicker chair that creaked like it knew how to hold grief. "And if you're here to tell me she's dead, you can leave."

I didn't sit.

"I'm not here to tell you that," I said softly. "I'm here to find the truth."

She looked at me then. Really looked. Something flickered. Recognition. Not of me— but of the way I said it. Like Yannis. Like someone who wasn't letting go.

She nodded once. Just once.

"I used to hear her walking the house, you know. After. For years. At night, soft steps down the corridor. Her door clicking shut. Then one day—nothing." She turned her head slightly. "You'd think silence would be peaceful. But peace... doesn't echo like that."

Ti-Sav's voice came gently. "Did Maïa ever talk about being afraid? Of anyone? Anything?"

A long pause.

"She never said. But she drew. Sometimes I'd find her in the garden, sketching leaves and bones and... things I didn't understand. One day she drew something and burned it before I could see. Said it wasn't for eyes." Shanta looked down at her hands. "That was two days before she left and never came back."

I stepped closer to the mantle, eyes on the banyan tree.

"Did she ever mention someone named Yannis?"

A pause.

"Once or twice, she trusted him because he was a good listener," Shanta said.

We stayed a while longer. Asked questions. Got half-answers. Everything weighed down by years of not saying too much, for fear the silence might crumble.

At the door, Shanta handed me something folded in yellowing cloth.

"It was under her bed. I couldn't bring myself to open it."

I didn't open it either. Not yet.

Some truths are still dreaming.

As we stepped back into the light, Ti-Sav exhaled.

"She never let herself say goodbye."

I looked back once at the quiet house.

"Maybe she's still waiting to say hello."

Chapter 48

The road from the Saramine house twisted through rain-slick bends and ghost-quiet cane fields. No one spoke. Not even Ti-Kiki, who usually filled silences with superstition or swearing. Tonight, there was only the soft grumble of the truck and the smell of damp leaves.

Amaya stared out the window, fingers pressed against her lips.

"She still washes Maïa's clothes like she is still there," Ti-Sav said finally.

Amaya nodded, barely. "That wasn't memory. That was belief."

"She asked if we were the police," Ti-Kiki said. "But not because she was scared of us. She was scared of what we'd *confirm*."

They passed a cluster of half-lit homes. A dog barked twice, then went quiet. The island felt like it was holding its breath.

"I thought it would bring her peace," Amaya whispered. "Showing her the cloth. The site. Letting her know we hadn't forgotten."

"And did it?" Ti-Sav asked.

"No," she said. "Because if Maïa's gone, her mother has to bury her again. And if she's alive—then why hasn't she come back?"

***

Back at the station, the light from Ravi's office spilled down the hall—dim, muted, still on.

"Didn't know he was here," Ti-Kiki muttered.

"He doesn't leave when he's afraid something's still out there," Amaya said.

She tapped the door.

"Come in," Ravi's voice called.

He was at his desk, scrolling through old files—paper ones. The edges yellowed, soft from years of flipping. He looked up, eyes shadowed but sharp.

"You found something," he said, not asking.

Amaya stepped forward. "You digitized part of Yannis' journal five years ago. Why?"

Ravi didn't flinch. "Because he asked me to. Not officially. But... he gave me a set of pages. Said if anything ever happened to him, I'd know what to look for."

Ti-Sav raised a brow. "And did you?"

He sighed. "Not then. Not until your last site visit. I saw the same mark on one of the diagrams he gave me."

He pulled open a drawer, lifted out a plastic sleeve.

Inside: a handwritten note. Same script as the warning they'd found.

You shouldn't go alone. Even if you hear them calling.

"I kept it," Ravi said. "Didn't know what to make of it back then. Thought it might be a fragment of folklore Yannis had copied. Now I think... it wasn't his handwriting. And I think it was meant for Maïa."

Amaya leaned closer. "Where did he find it?"

"Behind a shrine near the Cascade d'Ambre. Hidden in a sealed glass jar, wrapped in oil cloth. It was already brittle."

Ti-Kiki crossed his arms. "You didn't think to follow up?"

Ravi met his gaze. "I did. But the shrine was empty. Burnt-out candles. No signs of anyone. I filed it under 'cultural debris.' I didn't connect it to Maïa. Not then."

Silence stretched. Heavy. Honest.

Then Ti-Sav said, "We go tomorrow. If the shrine's still there."

Amaya nodded, but didn't take her eyes off Ravi.

"I want to work with people I can trust," she said quietly. "The island's not giving us second chances."

Ravi's jaw tightened. "I know."

He didn't apologize again. Didn't explain.

He just reached for the case file and opened it between them.

And for now, that was enough.

Chapter 49

The cascade was louder than memory.

Not the roaring kind of loud—but a steady, rhythmic hum that filled the trees, the moss, the air. Like the island was exhaling in its sleep.

We stood at the edge of the glade, boots pressed into the damp earth, where a path barely visible wove its way toward the rocks. Ti-Sav moved ahead, machete slicing through hanging vines.

"You said the shrine was here?" she asked.

Ravi nodded, slow. "Near the base. Carved into the rock shelf."

Kiki grumbled behind us. "We shouldn't be here on a waning moon. Water spirits get twitchy."

"Everything gets twitchy when we get too close," I murmured.

The shrine was still there—but barely.

Moss had crept over the stones. Half the votive bowls had cracked under rain and sun. The small shelf where offerings once stood had collapsed, but the base—etched into basalt—still bore faint outlines.

A lotus.

And the glyph.

Not carved. Burned in. The edges blackened as if a flame had kissed only that shape.

Ti-Sav crouched. "There was something here. A jar, maybe. Hollowed space under the ledge."

Ravi crouched beside her. "I found it almost five years ago. Thought it was just ritual leftovers. I kept the note because it felt...off."

"Off how?" I asked.

He paused. "It wasn't island writing. Too modern. The ink was smudged but there was a signature. Not a name. Just... Z."

Kiki's eyes narrowed. "Z as in ZakaLand?"

"Z as in something trying to be a myth," I muttered.

We all went quiet again.

Then Ti-Sav said, "There's wax here."

She held up her gloves—scraping bits of dark red wax from the hollow.

"Candle or seal?" I asked.

She sniffed. "Not candle. Smells like cinnamon. Like a ward."

Ravi stood up, wiping his palms on his pants. "We missed it. Whatever they wanted hidden, it's long gone."

"But they marked it," I said, running my fingers over the glyph. "They left a trail."

"Question is," said Kiki, "did they want us to follow it?"

"Or did they want us to follow it straight into silence?"

Chapter 50

The walls of the station buzzed low with humidity and old secrets. Ravi stood at the whiteboard, arms folded, eyes narrowed at the constellation of names, dates, and properties they'd strung together over weeks.

Jean-Yves Laforme. Always there in the margins. Never the centre.

Until now.

"We triple-checked," Ti-Sav said, tapping the photo with her pen. "Bank deposits, offshore holding ties, deleted internal drives. It all curves back to him."

Amaya scanned the document trail—each one a breadcrumb dropped in quiet desperation. "So why now?"

"Because guilt has a shelf life," Ravi muttered. "And someone needed him quiet long enough to finish the job."

"Or," Ti-Kiki added from the corner, "he's finally the weak link in a chain that thinks it's unbreakable."

They didn't say it out loud, but they all felt it. Jean-Yves wasn't the top. He was the hinge.

***

The house smelled like rum and second chances gone stale. A bungalow in the Bel Arbre quarter, tucked behind frangipani hedges and washed-out political posters from an election nobody won.

Ravi knocked. Once. Then twice.

Jean-Yves opened the door barefoot, blinking in the morning light. He looked older than his official age. Not in the bones, but in the breath.

"You brought the cavalry," he said, eyeing the team.

"No," said Ravi. "We brought the facts."

He stepped aside without a word.

****

Inside, the air was too quiet. The kind of silence that had lived there for years.

Photos lined the mantle—his children, birthdays, one blurry snapshot of a young girl with curls and mischief. Maia? No. His daughter. The resemblance made Amaya stop.

"I kept it all," Jean-Yves said from behind them. "The files. The plans. I thought... maybe one day someone would ask."

"And now we are," Ti-Sav said.

He sat down slowly on the edge of the sofa, hands trembling just enough.

"I didn't kill her," he said. "But I buried the truth."

"And why now?" Ravi asked.

He looked at the photo again. "Because my daughter just turned seventeen."

Nobody spoke.

Because that was enough.

Chapter 51

The interrogation room smelled like bleach and old lies.

Jean-Yves sat with his jacket off, shirt rumpled, eyes dull. He didn't ask for a lawyer. He didn't even ask for water.

He just stared at his hands, fingers twitching slightly.

Amaya sat across from him. Ravi stood against the wall, arms crossed. Ti-Sav leaned in the doorway, arms folded.

No one spoke at first.

Until Amaya slid the photo forward.

The one from the wooden box.

Maïa. Seventeen. Standing by the banyan tree. Behind her, a shadow that shouldn't be there.

Jean-Yves looked at it and exhaled like he'd been holding the truth in his lungs for twenty years.

"I didn't kill her," he said.

"Who did?" Amaya asked.

He didn't answer.

"You said you wanted your children to know who you really were," Ravi said. "So, tell us."

Jean-Yves rubbed his forehead. "I knew about the land. I didn't know about her. Not at first."

"What land?" Ti-Sav asked.

"The sites. The ones we marked. Old family records. They said there were... deposits. Colonial artefacts. Wealth moved off-books. Hidden before the Independence push."

"And the glyphs?" Amaya asked.

He blinked. "I didn't draw them."

"Someone did."

He hesitated. "There was a man. Not Luc. Older. Part of the group. He said the glyphs marked the blood locks. Places sealed with a promise."

Ravi's voice was low. "A soul promise?"

Jean-Yves nodded, pale now. "That's what he called it."

"And Maïa?"

"She saw too much. Took something. Notes, sketches, maybe a map. I don't know. She went quiet after that. One of the others said she was dealt with."

"And you didn't ask?" Amaya snapped.

He looked at her. Just looked. "You think people like me ask questions when our name is on the land deeds? When the money's flowing?"

Amaya leaned forward. "Someone buried her."

Jean-Yves shook his head. "No. Someone buried what she knew."

A pause.

Then softly, "There was a rule among us: 'If the island doesn't speak of it, neither do we.'"

He looked at the photo again.

"She should've never been there. But none of us should've either."

Ravi stepped forward. "Names. Who else was part of it?"

Jean-Yves laughed. It was bitter and small. "You still think they'll go down with me?"

He met Ravi's eyes.

"They were born with the island's secrets in their blood. I was just trying to buy a bigger house."

Chapter 52

The prison interview room smelled like bleach and resignation.

Jean-Yves sat opposite them—wrists cuffed, shirt wrinkled, eyes hollow. A man who'd spent years laundering guilt through silence. Now, nothing to iron it flat.

Amaya placed the photo on the table.

Maïa. Two men. One blurred face. One Jean-Yves couldn't deny.

He didn't look at it.

"You left her there," she said quietly.

He blinked. Once. Twice.

"I didn't kill her," he whispered.

"No," said Ravi. "But you watched."

Silence again.

Then Jean-Yves' voice cracked open like rotting wood:

"They said she'd gone too far. That she'd stolen something. But it wasn't theft. It was curiosity."

"She took something?" Amaya asked.

Jean-Yves nodded slowly. "A folded paper. Old. Looked like a map. They dropped it. She picked it up."

Jean-Yves shifts uncomfortably. "They told me to follow her. Just... watch. Said she might try to talk."

"And?" Amaya asks, voice steady.

"She started avoiding them. I think she knew something."

Jean-Yves' voice drops. "She wasn't like the others. She didn't scare easy."

"What did she know?" Amaya asked.

He hesitated, then said, "I don't know what she saw. But a few days before she vanished, she said something I can't forget."

They waited.

"She said, 'They're not digging to build. They're digging to take back what was never theirs.'"

Chapter 53

The interrogation room had emptied, but the air still held the shape of Jean-Yves' confession. Amaya sat on the station's back steps, knees pulled to her chest, the night pressed close. Behind her, the hallway buzzed faintly with too many whispered theories and not enough facts.

Ti-Sav joined her, two mugs in hand. "You okay?"

"Define okay."

Ti-Sav handed her the cup. "You were right. There was more. Always more."

They sat in silence a while, sipping the tea that tasted faintly of burnt ginger and salt. Amaya stared at the stars, but all she could see were the ruins—literal and otherwise.

"He didn't kill her," she said finally. "But he handed her over. That makes him a link in the chain."

"And the others?" Ti-Sav asked. "The real orchestrators?"

Amaya shook her head. "Names like Garnier, Lajoie, Chazan... They're not going to give us files. They *are* the files. The system's woven around them."

Ti-Sav blew on her tea. "You ever wonder what would've happened if Maïa had left that day?"

"I think she tried. I think the moment she realized what she'd stumbled into, she didn't just want to run. She wanted to *stop* it. And maybe... she left a trail."

"Like breadcrumbs?"

"Like glyphs."

They looked up at the wind-chimed silence.

Then Ravi's voice called from the hallway. "You need to see this."

✳✳✳

The evidence board in the small conference room had grown teeth. Amaya stepped closer. A new photograph had been tacked in the corner — recent, smudged, timestamped from the coast guard.

A wooden crate. Washed up near Trou d'Emeraude. Half-buried in coral sand. Cracked open.

Inside: coins, rusted tools, fragments of chain, a child's anklet.

Carved into the wood, barely visible — the same glyph. Slashed into the panel like it had been trying to get out.

"Found it this morning," Ravi said. "Hurricane currents shifted a sand bar."

"Treasure?" Ti-Sav asked.

"Grave," Amaya corrected.

Ravi tapped a second image: a blurry black-and-white scan from the old colonial archive. Same crest. Same mark. *Soul promise.*

Ti-Kiki ambled in, rum bottle half-corked. "Island's coughing up what it doesn't want to carry."

"No," Amaya said quietly. "It's giving us a chance to *see* it. Finally."

The room went still.

Then she whispered, "We're not just solving murders. We're standing in the middle of a reckoning."

Chapter 54

The café was almost empty.

Morning sun filtered through the shutters, striping the floor with lazy light. The smell of coffee and fried gato pima lingered, warm and grounding. Ravi knew the owner. Had known him since they both had black hair and fewer regrets. He didn't expect anyone else to be sitting at the back table.

But someone was.

Polished cufflinks. Pale linen shirt. No sweat despite the heat. He had the kind of face that didn't belong to anyone and yet knew too much.

Ravi didn't sit. "You're not on my calendar."

The man smiled without showing teeth. "We don't need calendars, Ravi. We've always been part of the same tide."

"I'm not much for swimming in circles."

"Then be careful you don't drown alone."

***

He didn't say his name. Didn't need to.

There were men on Zaka who spoke for the interests that didn't sign letters. Whose family names funded scholarships and land reclamation projects and also disappeared files. One of them was sitting here, sipping his tea like this was just another Thursday.

"You're interfering in things you used to know how to avoid," the man said. "And I get it. You're tired. Angry. You lost something."

Ravi's jaw tightened.

"You don't want to be the one they blame when the foundation cracks. But you also don't want to fall in with people who don't know how the island really breathes."

Ravi's hand curled slowly on the chair in front of him.

"So, this is the speech?" he asked. "The 'walk away while you still can't bit?"

"No," said the man. "This is the reminder."

He slid a small envelope across the table. Cream. Thick. No writing.

"I know what's in there," Ravi said without touching it.

"Good. Then you know what staying quiet looks like."

He rose. Buttoned his jacket. Smiled a smile that wasn't meant to reach anyone.

Then paused.

"Oh. And if you think your new friends will keep you safe—think again. One of them is already being watched."

And then he was gone.

***

Ravi didn't open the envelope.

He didn't need to. He knew what was inside.

A photo from long ago. One he thought he'd burned.

One that reminded him that no matter how far he'd come, the island remembered the version of him he wanted buried.

He left the café without finishing his coffee.

It was time to choose.

No more shadows.

No more fence.

And no more ghosts pretending to be friends.

Chapter 55

The community hall in Bel Zaka hadn't seen this much tension since the sugar subsidy hearings. Now, it buzzed with something sharper.

A town meeting, they said. Public transparency, they claimed. Really, it was an unofficial inquest—Zaka-style. Word had spread. Developers gone. Sacred lands sold. Bodies turning up. Rumours flying like crows before a storm.

Amaya sat in the front row, arms folded, eyes sharp. Ti-Sav leaned on the wall nearby, gaze scanning the crowd. Kiki was... well, somewhere, probably eating boiled peanuts and giving side commentary.

And at the centre of the makeshift stage, Ravi stepped forward.

No uniform today. Just a dark shirt, sleeves rolled, rosary bead bracelet on one wrist.

The hall fell quiet.

Ravi let the silence stretch. Then:

"I'm Inspector Ravi Caderamen. Some of you know me. Some of you think you do."

A ripple.

"I've served this island twenty-six years. I've shut up when I should've spoken. I've looked away when I should've looked harder. Because I thought I was protecting something bigger than me."

He paused. Breath in. Voice firm.

"I was wrong."

A louder murmur now.

"There's been a pattern of land grabs, of sacred sites desecrated for profit. There are murders, not accidents. There are coverups, not coincidences. And the people who benefit most have names that never show up in our reports. That ends today."

A woman near the back stood. "You saying this to us now—what does it mean?"

Ravi looked around the hall. Looked at Amaya. At Ti-Sav.

"It means I'm not hiding anymore. I'm with them. I'm with the truth. And if that means going down—so be it. But I won't be complicit. Not one more second."

Amaya exhaled slowly. Ti-Sav gave a single nod.

The crowd was quiet for a long moment.

Then someone clapped.

Then another.

And another.

It wasn't thunderous. Not yet. But it was *real*.

Ravi stepped back from the mic. He didn't smile.

But a weight lifted.

He was no longer walking between.

He'd chosen.

Chapter 56

"They clapped for you, Ravi. That scares them more than anybody we found."

The aftershock was quiet—but sharp.

Ravi's speech had barely cooled before the phone started buzzing. Media inquiries. Internal "check-ins." A message from the Commissioner: *We need to talk*. He ignored it.

Back at the station, the mood was split down the middle. Some of the junior officers nodded quietly when he passed. Others avoided his gaze like it might set them on fire.

Mervin wasn't avoiding anyone.

He walked into the breakroom like it was a courtroom.

"You really went full messiah, huh?" he said, pouring himself coffee. "Didn't think you had it in you."

Ravi didn't look up. "You were there."

"I was." Mervin sipped, shrugged. "Impressive. Bold. Dramatic. Completely derails every containment protocol we've been told to maintain."

"So, it needed derailing."

Mervin's smile didn't reach his eyes. "You're on your own now, Ravi. No shield. No favours. The people you just exposed? They won't forget."

"I'm counting on that."

Mervin studied him for a long moment, then leaned in slightly.

"You want to be a hero, fine. But don't expect the island to stay quiet. You dug into the soil. Now the roots are moving."

***

Amaya read the article twice later that night at Ti-Sav's apartment.

"Local Inspector Denounces Land Corruption in Public Meeting"

—The headline was cautious. The story wasn't.

"They published it," she whispered. "They actually ran it."

Ti-Sav looked over her shoulder. "They had to. Too many phones, too many eyes. Can't suppress something once it leaks like this."

"Still." Amaya exhaled. "It's begun."

Ti-Sav nodded. "Yeah. But what we *don't* know is how they'll respond. They won't just vanish. They'll adapt. Retaliate."

"And Mervin?"

Ti-Sav gave a wicked little grin. "He's rattled. He's still in play, but for the first time, he's off balance. He blinked."

***

Meanwhile in a dark office in Port Princess, shutters were drawn. One desk lamp casting light on a bottle of whiskey and a half-burned dossier.

A voice on the phone, tight and venomous:

"Get me the names of everyone who stood beside him. Everyone. I don't care if they're interns or old men selling peanuts on the beach. If they clapped, I want them watched."

Pause.

"And start digging into the girl. Zarin. If she doesn't back off soon..."

Click.

Chapter 57

Back at the borrowed room above Ti-Kiki's rum shack, the war room had taken shape. A whiteboard cluttered with glyph sketches, names, timelines. Yannis' journal opened like a gospel. Photos pinned with salt-stained tape. Red string optional, but emotionally present.

Ti-Sav clicked her pen. "We're not waiting for them to move. We're predicting it. They'll push back through two paths: discredit or disappearance."

Amaya nodded. "We get ahead of it. Map the vulnerable entry points."

"Ravi's past?" Ti-Sav asked.

"Too well-known," Amaya said. "Any dirt would've surfaced already. But us? We're the easier targets."

Kiki lit a clove cigarette by the window, muttering, "They'll try to spin it. Call it a political stunt. Blame it on a *foreign-trained hysteria specialist with a vendetta against her own island.*'" He winked at Amaya. "Cute title, no?"

She didn't smile. "We protect each other. We document everything. And we leak only when it hits critical mass."

"What about the Saramines?" Ti-Sav asked.

Amaya's jaw clenched. "We don't involve them unless we have no other choice. They've already buried one daughter."

Silence settled for a moment.

Then Kiki said, "So what's our next lead?"

Ti-Sav tapped the board. "We go to the old registry records. Land claims and transfer deeds from the colonial handover. Something's been hidden there. Luc wasn't the first. Just the latest."

Amaya nodded. "Follow the land. Follow the lies."

✳✳✳

Low voices discussion was held somewhere in an air-conditioned villa with marble floors.

At the head of the table sat a woman no one publicly named, but whose signature moved funding faster than Parliament.

"We underestimated the Inspector," she said, swirling ice in a tumbler of neat rum. "That was our mistake."

One of the men leaned forward. "We've begun seeding new articles. Painted him as a fading idealist clinging to ghosts. The 'colonial trauma narrative' plays well online."

"Not enough," she said. "This isn't just about the dead girl. It's about the map."

They all turned to her.

She dropped a single word: "Vault."

Another voice, colder: "You think it's real?"

She raised a brow. "I *know* what they buried."

A pause.

"Then what do we do?"

She leaned forward, deadly calm.

"We erase the map. We erase the bones. And if necessary—"

Her eyes glinted.

"—we erase the island's memory."

Chapter 58

The AC was too cold for island bones. Ravi sat in a room that smelled like new laminate and old paranoia. The walls were bare. The clock ticked too loud. No badge on the desk—just a manila file and a recording device.

Across from him sat Commissioner Seraphin, flanked by Deputy Doyen, eyes unreadable.

"Inspector Caderamen," Seraphin began, not unkindly. "We're not here to punish integrity. But your public statement—let's call it... unconventional."

Ravi didn't speak.

"You've served this department with distinction for over twenty years," Doyen added, as if reciting from a eulogy. "But this isn't the first time your methods have drawn attention."

A pause.

Then: "Do you still believe you're the right person to lead this investigation?"

Ravi looked them both in the eye. "Do you still believe it's just an investigation?"

The room went still.

Seraphin tapped the file. "The Ministry is concerned your... emotional proximity may be clouding your judgment. You were seen with Dr. Zarin. Off-duty. On multiple occasions."

Ravi leaned forward. "You mean doing my job?"

"Is it your job to bring down ZakaLand Holdings? To make speeches that implicate names not in evidence?" Doyen's voice was sharper now.

Ravi didn't blink. "I think it's my job not to look away."

Another pause. Longer. Heavier.

Seraphin finally spoke. "We won't remove you. Not yet. But you'll submit your next findings for departmental review. No press. No sidebars. No more speeches."

"And if I don't?"

"Then we both know what comes next."

Ravi stood. "No. You don't."

Chapter 59

The first article dropped at dawn.

A glossy piece from a mainland paper with Zaka's official logo faint in the background. Headline: "Forensics or Folklore? Foreign-Trained Consultant Accused of Bias in Island Investigations."

They'd used an old photo of Amaya — sharp suit, tired eyes, standing beside an excavation pit in Oxfordshire. But the caption read: *"Controversial outsider Dr. Zarin under scrutiny for unsubstantiated cultural claims."*

Ravi tossed the paper onto the police station's table, jaw clenched. "They're moving fast."

Amaya stared at it for a second too long. "They called me a mainlander with mainland theories. Convenient."

Ti-Sav scrolled on her phone. "They're reposting it everywhere. With hashtags. Even got Mervin's 'anonymous source' on air — talking about professional misconduct."

Kiki chewed his gato piment slowly. "If they can't bury the bodies, they'll try to bury your credibility."

"Discredit the woman, not the findings," Ravi muttered. "Same playbook. Different generation."

And then came the letter.

Delivered in an unmarked envelope to Amaya's guesthouse. No return address. Just a smear of clove oil on the flap.

Inside, one line, scrawled in red ink:

"Some graves were meant to stay closed."

She didn't flinch.

But when she folded the note and slipped it into her bag, her hands were steady with rage.

Chapter 60

The meeting wasn't official. No minutes. No uniforms. Just the four of them and the island breathing outside the windows.

"We've stirred something deep," Ti-Sav said, fingers clenched around her mug. "I got a call last night. Not from HQ. From my mother. Asking if I'm safe. Someone got to her."

Ti-Kiki grunted. "Same here. My cousin's rum license? Suspended. No reason. Just gone."

Amaya looked at them both. "They're trying to starve us quietly."

Ravi leaned back. "My file's been flagged for review. Internal affairs. Nothing concrete — just enough to stain."

For a second, no one spoke. The silence was filled with everything they couldn't say.

Then Ravi cleared his throat. "We can step back. We can wait. Let the fire burn low."

Ti-Sav shook her head. "And let them write the ending again?"

Ti-Kiki's voice was low but firm. "This station's my family. And if they come for my family, I come for them."

Ravi looked at Amaya. "You still in?"

She didn't blink. "I don't have anyone left to lose."

A beat passed.

Then she added, "But I have too many dead who never got the truth."

Ravi stood up. "Then we go forward."

Ti-Sav nodded, shoulders squared. "Together."

And just like that, the line was drawn.

Chapter 61

Ti-Sav had just finished logging the cloth sample updates when her phone buzzed.

Unknown number. One line. No punctuation.

"Bel Rivage site off limits at night ask deva 2016 incident"

She stared at it for a long minute.

Then she called Amaya.

***

Ti-Sav and Amaya met behind the former Bel Rivage hotel ruins. The sea was loud. So was Ti-Kiki's voice as he argued with a stray cat near the fence.

"Deva was a site supervisor back in 2016," Ti-Sav explained. "Quit after a breakdown. Claimed 'the spirits didn't want them there.' Got dismissed as rum hallucinations."

Amaya raised an eyebrow. "And now?"

"We find Deva."

***

Ti-Sav found her outside a coconut oil processing plant in Souillac. Name tag: Deva Bissondoyal. Nervous hands. Smelled faintly of lemongrass and something harder.

She blinked when Ti-Sav showed her badge. "You people again?"

"We're not here to question your mental health," Ti-Sav said gently. "We're here because you saw something."

A pause. Then:

"They built at night," Deva said. "The workers weren't local. They spoke French. Not Zakais French. Rich-boy French."

"Where?"

"Behind Bel Rivage. Past the old banyan. They said it was a utility substation. But I saw crates. Big ones. And they wouldn't let anyone near the second chamber."

"What chamber?"

"The one underground. You think the vault is treasure?" Her voice cracked. "It's worse. They weren't hiding gold. They were burying shame."

Ti-Sav leaned forward. "Why come forward now?"

Deva looked away. "Because I saw the speech. And I thought maybe someone was finally listening."

***

The drone launched just after dawn. Lior, Ti-Kiki's techie nephew, controlled it from the back of his van with a half-eaten gato piment in hand. The jungle shimmered with dew and suspicion.

The footage wasn't impressive at first— trees, shadows, an abandoned utility shack.

Then— A wide depression in the earth. Rectangular. Too clean.

A break in the canopy.

Faint markings in the clearing's dirt— almost like... a grid.

Amaya squinted at the screen. "No one builds like this without planning. Or hiding."

Lior nodded. "I mapped the GPS. Cross-references with ZakaLand's old permits from 2017. But they never declared any construction here."

Ti-Kiki frowned. "And they never meant to."

Chapter 62

We moved at first light.

No sirens. No uniforms. Just boots, breath, and the hum of something that felt too much like dread. The jungle near the site was dense, tangled with vines and old intentions.

Ravi led. Ti-Sav watched our backs. I had the map and the flashlight, both flickering.

We reached the clearing faster than expected. The trees parted like they'd been told to behave. Ahead, the structure from the drone footage rose out of the ground — half-hidden under corrugated sheets and tarpaulins. No signage. No noise.

And no reason for it to be here.

"Smells like fresh concrete," Ti-Sav muttered. "But there's no road access."

"Exactly," Ravi said. "Whatever this is, it was built to be forgotten."

We circled the perimeter. Ti-Kiki had slipped away somewhere, muttering about "bad ground and worse spirits." Can't say I disagreed.

Ravi found it first — a ventilation shaft, tucked beneath thick brush. Industrial. Fresh. Someone had thought they could mask it with ferns and distance.

I kneeled beside it. Cold air leaked up.

"Underground," I said.

Ravi's voice was a whisper. "They didn't just bury treasures. They built a vault to keep them breathing."

And then we heard it.

Movement below.

Not rats.

Not pipes.

Footsteps.

Chapter 63

We pulled back from the shaft, ducking into the brush.

Ti-Sav tapped her comm. "Drone still circling?"

A crackle. Lior's voice: "Copy. No visible movement topside. But I picked up heat signatures—three. Maybe four. Underground."

I exhaled. "So not abandoned."

"Worse," Ti-Kiki said, reappearing with a lit clove cigarette and a machete that hadn't been clean since 2003. "Guarded."

Ravi crouched, sketching something in the dirt — shaft, possible entrances, terrain. His jaw was clenched tight. The way it always was when the mask of protocol cracked and the man underneath remembered why he stayed in Zaka.

"Entry through the vent's too narrow," he said. "Main structure is sealed. We need access without spooking them."

Ti-Sav nodded. "A silent breach. Or… bait."

Kiki grinned. "You volunteering?"

"I'm thinking," she said dryly, "we let them think we're clueless. We get eyes on every angle first."

Amaya's gaze was locked on the ventilation shaft. "Someone's down there guarding something they're willing to kill for. But they don't expect we've already seen them."

"They think Zaka sleeps," Ravi said.

"But Zaka watches," Kiki replied.

Silence settled again, the kind that wasn't empty — just waiting.

Then Amaya whispered, "We don't go in yet. We watch. We listen. And when we move..."

Ti-Sav finished it: "We move like ghosts."

Chape

Chapter 64

The next twelve hours passed in shifts.

Kiki and Lior rigged up motion sensors, low-light cams, and a signal scrambler Ti-Kiki swore he got "from a friend with no fingerprints." They set them like breadcrumbs around the jungle perimeter.

Ti-Sav mapped heat signatures to a crude overlay of the terrain. "Four bodies still moving. Pattern is tight. No signs of panic — they don't know we're here."

"Or they don't care," Amaya muttered.

Ravi didn't speak much. But every time he passed the sketch he'd drawn earlier, he updated it — refining the angles, repositioning the guards. Building a plan in silence.

By sunset, tension was a living thing.

Then: a ping.

Lior's voice crackled through. "Movement outside. One heading northeast. Fast."

Ti-Sav bolted upright. "Scout?"

Kiki shook his head. "Or a runner."

"Let's tail him," Ravi said. "Not stop — track. See who he's going to."

***

They moved silent through the underbrush. Amaya counted footfalls and timed their spacing. Whoever it was, he knew the land. Too confident for a new recruit.

Twenty minutes in, the runner stopped at a clearing. Pulled out a satellite phone.

Amaya froze. "That's not local tech."

They watched as he spoke quickly, then snapped the phone shut and crushed it under his boot.

Ravi tapped Amaya's arm. "He's heading west. Toward the sugarcane."

Her stomach tightened.

"That's near the old well," she said. "Where the land dips. The one Yannis marked."

***

By the time they returned to hidden base, Ti-Sav's fingers were flying across her tablet.

"That path? It skirts near the old mill compound — the one ZL fenced off in 2019. No permits filed, no access logs."

Ti-Sav looked up. "Why does every dirty thread lead back to that company?"

Chapter 65

The rain had stopped sometime before dawn, but the air was still thick with that Zaka damp—mud and moss and something older. Like the island knew what we were about to find.

The entrance lay beneath layers of camouflage. What looked like overgrowth was a tarp, faded and slick. Beneath it: concrete. Reinforced. Seamless. Not abandoned.

Ti-Sav ran a hand along the edge, frowning. "This wasn't made in a day."

"No," Ravi said, his voice low. "Or by amateurs."

Amaya crouched beside the vent. "Still no sound?"

Kiki nodded once. "Shadows shifting inside. They're trying to stay quiet. Not quiet enough."

The drone had mapped the perimeter. Four guards, no insignia. Clean boots. Military posture. Not locals. Whoever they were, they'd been paid to protect something invisible. Something heavy.

"We breach from the blind side," Ravi said. "Silent, surgical."

"Doors?" Amaya asked.

"One." He pointed on the sketch. "Coded. But old. Could've been installed years ago and forgotten by everyone except the right people."

Kiki grunted. "Forgotten doesn't mean unguarded."

Ti-Sav pulled out the equipment—signal dampeners, glass-cutters, old-school tools for old-school secrets.

"Once we're in, no hero moves," she said. "We document. We pull evidence. We get out."

"And if someone's inside?" Amaya asked.

Ravi met her eyes. "We warn them. Once."

Kiki rolled his shoulders. "And if they don't listen?"

"Then we show them Zaka remembers."

They moved into position.

As Amaya took one last look toward the treeline, something flickered behind her ribs—a memory, not quite hers.

The glyph.

The silence.

The space under the ground where voices were never meant to echo.

She whispered, "Let's bring the ghosts into the light."

And the vault waited.

Chapter 66

The plan wasn't written. It was felt.

No sirens. No backup. Just four people who didn't like what the island whispered when it thought no one was listening.

Ravi adjusted the strap of his sidearm. "Lior confirmed the timing. Guards rotate every hour. There's a five-minute window between the last one leaving and the next arriving."

Ti-Sav checked her watch. "Ten minutes to go."

Kiki spat into the grass. "I hate waiting."

"We're not waiting," Amaya said. "We're aligning."

***

The entrance wasn't glamorous. Just a sliver in the ground behind a corrugated shack, half-covered with rotting palm fronds and guilt. The kind of place no tourist brochure would dare mention.

Ti-Sav popped the latch with a rusted crowbar. The metal groaned like it was mourning.

They went down one by one.

The air turned thick, wet, still. Like breathing inside someone else's lungs.

Kiki muttered, "This place smells like bad secrets."

Amaya led the way, flashlight dancing across stone and shadow. Glyphs — the real ones, old and eroded — carved into support beams. Not for design. For direction.

Ravi whispered, "They weren't building over sacred ground…"

"They were tunnelling into it," Amaya finished.

***

The vault wasn't just a vault.

Not a bunker of concrete and secrets. Not merely a stash of old wealth.

It was a monument to silence. To what power feared and still hoarded anyway.

The walls were lined with locked cabinets and glass display cases — some holding rusted blades, bone carvings, colonial relics stripped from sacred land. Others held things harder to name. Shards of what looked like ritual tools.

A child's bracelet. A book bound in palm fibre and faded ink.

And in the far corner: a glass case.

Inside it, under a spotlight: a photo.

Maïa.

Seventeen. Hair wild, eyes defiant. Flanked by two men — their faces blurred from age or design.

Ti-Sav stepped closer. "This shouldn't be here."

Amaya didn't move. Her voice was low, strained. "This was a vault. But not just for things."

"For stories," Ravi said. "For threats. For memories they wanted to keep... but couldn't let escape."

"And Maïa?" Ti-Kiki asked.

"She saw something. Maybe more than once. Maybe she took something. A drawing. A map. A name. Enough to scare them." Amaya's hand hovered over the glass, not touching. "This photo... this was their way of keeping her locked in even after she vanished."

Ti-Sav's jaw clenched. "Like a warning."

"Like a trophy," Amaya replied. "Proof that even silence can be collected."

They didn't find a body. No burial. No bones.

Just that image, framed like art. Preserved like a threat.

The island groaned faintly through the stone under their feet.

Amaya whispered, "We were never chasing a killer. We were chasing what power does when it's afraid of being seen."

Ravi didn't speak.

He just lifted the ledger beside the photo.

On the first page: List of Initiates.

The last name scrawled at the bottom: Jean-Yves Laroche.

And next to it—

A single line in red ink:

The island remembers. And so must we.

Chapter 67

They started with the ones they could touch.

The three guards taken in the raid cracked faster than expected. Not loyalty—just fear. Fear of being the last one holding the match when the blaze started swallowing buildings.

François Karam folded first. Too many land deeds in his name. Too many late-night transfers. Too many calls to lawyers who stopped answering.

He named names.

Some already listed in the ledger.

Some not.

The list of initiates stretched back over six decades. Names faded with time. Some crossed out. Some marked with symbols Amaya didn't recognize. A circle. A flame. A slash.

But the most damning part wasn't who was on it.

It was who still lived.

Three active government officials.

One media baron.

A philanthropist who'd once been shortlisted for the Zakan Peace Medal.

And a foreign "consultant" with dual passports and holdings in Nevis, Guernsey, and Vanuatu.

"We tried following the money," Ti-Sav said, laying a sheet of banking data on the table. "But it's like tracing water in the desert."

Routing chains, shell companies, blacklisted tax havens. ZakaLand Holdings was just one spoke on a wheel too big to turn without breaking it.

"We won't get them all," Ravi said.

"But we'll get the ones the island still remembers," Amaya replied.

Ti-Kiki lit a clove cigarette. "And the rest?"

"They'll feel the heat," said Ravi. "Whether justice touches them or just their reputation."

Chapter 68

By noon, the names had leaked.

No one said who let them out. But everyone knew.

Ti-Kiki swore it wasn't him. Which probably meant it was.

The press went wild first. Local journalists, long silenced by funding ties and invisible threats, found their spine. Screens lit up with images of arrest warrants, redacted ledger entries, and blurred photos of vault rooms full of gold and bones.

But it wasn't just a headline anymore.

It was personal.

In marketplaces and backstreets, people stopped pretending. Mothers wept. Elders shook their heads. Young ones, raised on half-truths, clenched fists and lit candles on street corners — not for protest. For mourning.

Mourning time lost. Friends vanished. Stories buried beneath concrete and colonial scars.

"They used us," Ti-Sav said, watching from the precinct window. "Fed us ghosts so they could steal the land."

"They fed us silence," Amaya said. "And sold our memory for profit."

Crowds gathered in front of the police station. Peaceful, but pulsing with fury.

Some held up signs: *"Zaka se rapel."*

Others held old photographs. A few clutched copies of Maia's last sketch — the one no one ever saw until now.

And then came the Saramines.

Maïa's parents.

Their eyes were tired. Hollow in places grief had carved years ago.

But they stood taller than Amaya remembered.

"We heard," her mother said simply.

Amaya didn't speak. She just stepped forward and held out the photo — the real one. The one found in the vault, behind the glass. Maïa between two men. Caught between fear and defiance.

"She fought," Amaya said. "She tried to stop them. And they buried her for it."

Her father's lips trembled, but he didn't cry.

"She was always too brave," he whispered. "We told her not to ask questions."

Silence.

Then, softly, her mother reached for the photo.

And held it like a daughter.

Chapter 67

The courtroom wasn't built for this many ghosts.

The trial stretched for weeks. Testimonies crackled through radios. Transcripts were leaked, redacted, corrected, and re-leaked.

Some of the accused pled guilty. Some wept. Most didn't.

The charges stuck to the weakest links. A few resignations. A few quiet deaths abroad. A handful of well-tailored monsters suddenly too sick to testify.

But the island remembered.

The real sentencing happened in whispers — at fruit stalls, bus stops, school gates.

"He was one of them."

"She knew what they were doing."

"Maïa warned us. We didn't listen."

***

Ravi stood taller at the final hearing.

Uniform crisp. Rosary still tucked at his belt.

He testified without bitterness, without glory. Just truth.

Later, he returned to the precinct. No brass band. No applause.

But the junior officers looked him in the eye now. And called him *Inspector* without a sneer.

He stayed.

***

Ti-Sav took over the community outreach.

Workshops. History sessions. Artifact recovery with context, not shame.

She made schoolchildren laugh while teaching them how bones talk. She planted trees at every sacred site they once tried to pave over.

***

And Amaya?

She went home.

Not London. Not even the station.

Home — to the windswept ridge above Port Princess. Yannis' favourite overlook.

The island opened below like a held breath.

She laid a new photo beside the old journal.

Maïa. Laughing in jasmine. Finally, back in the light.

Amaya whispered, "We remembered."

She didn't expect an answer.

But the wind lifted.

Warm. Salted. Like sugarcane smoke.

And the trees below leaned ever so slightly.

Like they were listening.

Epilogue

Six months later, Zaka breathed differently.

The island still held its secrets, but now they weren't all buried.

Tourists came. But they walked slower, listened longer. Guides told fuller stories. Some of them hurt. Some of them healed.

A new exhibit opened in the old colonial customs house.

"Things We Were Told to Forget."

Bones, artifacts, a replica of the glyph carved in basalt. One of Maïa's sketches on a plinth, the paper sealed in glass. It showed a banyan split down the middle — roots reaching in both directions.

Ravi stood beside Amaya on opening day. No fanfare, just quiet pride.

"They'll try again," he said. "Maybe not the same men. But someone."

She nodded. "Then we keep remembering louder."

He smiled. "You staying?"

"For now," she said.

Later, she walked through Yannis' house. No ghosts. Just echoes.

She opened a window. Let in the warm night, the sound of frogs, a distant drumbeat.

Outside, kids played under the mango tree. One traced a shape in the dirt with a stick — looping, careful.

A circle. Then flame.

Amaya didn't stop her.

Some stories need to burn through to start again.

The End